Edgar Wallace was born illegitimat
adopted by George Freeman, a porte.
eleven, Wallace sold newspapers at Ludgate Circus and on leaving
school took a job with a printer. He enlisted in the Royal West Kent
Regiment, later transferring to the Medical Staff Corps and was sent
to South Africa. In 1898 he published a collection of poems called
The Mission that Failed, left the army and became a correspondent
for Reuters.

Wallace became the South African war correspondent for *The
Daily Mail*. His articles were later published as *Unofficial Dispatches* and
his outspokenness infuriated Kitchener, who banned him as a war
correspondent until the First World War. He edited the *Rand Daily
Mail*, but gambled disastrously on the South African Stock Market,
returning to England to report on crimes and hanging trials. He
became editor of *The Evening News*, then in 1905 founded the Tallis
Press, publishing *Smith*, a collection of soldier stories, and *Four Just
Men*. At various times he worked on *The Standard*, *The Star*, *The Week-
End Racing Supplement* and *The Story Journal*.

In 1917 he became a Special Constable at Lincoln's Inn and also
a special interrogator for the War Office. His first marriage to Ivy
Caldecott, daughter of a missionary, had ended in divorce and he
married his much younger secretary, Violet King.

The Daily Mail sent Wallace to investigate atrocities in the Belgian
Congo, a trip that provided material for his *Sanders of the River* books.
In 1923 he became Chairman of the Press Club and in 1931 stood as
a Liberal candidate at Blackpool. On being offered a scriptwriting
contract at RKO, Wallace went to Hollywood. He died in 1932, on
his way to work on the screenplay for *King Kong*.

THE ADMIRABLE CARFEW

THE ANGEL OF TERROR

THE AVENGER (USA: THE HAIRY ARM)

BIG FOOT

THE BLACK ABBOT

BONES

BONES IN LONDON

BONES OF THE RIVER

THE CLUE OF THE NEW PIN

THE CLUE OF THE SILVER KEY

THE CLUE OF THE TWISTED CANDLE

THE COAT OF ARMS (USA: THE ARRANWAYS MYSTERY)

THE COUNCIL OF JUSTICE

THE CRIMSON CIRCLE

THE DAFFODIL MYSTERY

THE DARK EYES OF LONDON (USA: THE CROAKERS)

THE DAUGHTERS OF THE NIGHT

A DEBT DISCHARGED

THE DEVIL MAN

THE DOOR WITH SEVEN LOCKS

THE DUKE IN THE SUBURBS

THE FACE IN THE NIGHT

THE FEATHERED SERPENT

THE FLYING SQUAD

THE FORGER (USA: THE CLEVER ONE)

THE FOUR JUST MEN

FOUR SQUARE JANE

THE FOURTH PLAGUE

THE FRIGHTENED LADY

GOOD EVANS

THE HAND OF POWER

THE IRON GRIP

THE JOKER (USA: THE COLOSSUS)

THE JUST MEN OF CORDOVA

THE KEEPERS OF THE KING'S PEACE

THE LAW OF THE FOUR JUST MEN

THE LONE HOUSE MYSTERY

THE MAN WHO BOUGHT LONDON

THE MAN WHO KNEW

THE MAN WHO WAS NOBODY

THE MIND OF MR J G REEDER (USA: THE MURDER BOOK OF J G REEDER)

MORE EDUCATED EVANS

MR J G REEDER RETURNS (USA: MR REEDER RETURNS)

MR JUSTICE MAXELL

RED ACES

ROOM 13

SANDERS

SANDERS OF THE RIVER

THE SINISTER MAN

THE SQUARE EMERALD (USA: THE GIRL FROM SCOTLAND YARD)

THE THREE JUST MEN

THE THREE OAK MYSTERY

THE TRAITOR'S GATE

WHEN THE GANGS CAME TO LONDON

Barbara on
her Own

HOUSE OF
STRATUS

This edition published in 2001 by House of Stratus, an imprint of Stratus Holdings plc, 24c Old Burlington Street, London, W1X 1RL, UK. Also at: Suite 210, 1270 Avenue of the Americas, New York, NY 10020, USA.

www.houseofstratus.com

Typeset, printed and bound by House of Stratus.

A catalogue record for this book is available from the British Library and the Library of Congress

ISBN 1-84232-660-0

We would like to thank the Edgar Wallace Society for all the support they have given House of Stratus. Enquiries on how to join the Edgar Wallace Society should be addressed to:
The Edgar Wallace Society, c/o Penny Wyrd, 84 Ridgefield Road, Oxford, OX4 3DA. Email: info@edgarwallace.org Web: http://www.edgarwallace.org/

1

On that day of fate, when, it seemed, nothing human could save the house of Maber & Maber from absorption by its rival; when the snowy façade of Atterman Brothers leered across the street at its stagnant competitor and said, as plainly as though the words were written in letters of brass, "You're my next annexe"; when Mr Maber himself was rather preoccupied by the dinner he was giving to the Cambridge crew than with the forthcoming dissolution of his century-old business: on that day of all days in the year Barbara Storr got out of bed the wrong side.

The bed was against the wall, so that really she could not get out any other way without damage to the brickwork. And as she dressed she thought, and Myrtle, seeing the frown on her face, wondered whether the bacon had been too salt, for she was a materialist who traced all human emotions to the eccentricities of digestion.

"Myrtle," said Barbara tragically, "I'm unpopular!"

"Lor', miss!" said Myrtle.

Her real name was Polly Oaks, but Barbara had views about names.

"I'm not only unpopular, but I'm darned unpopular," said Barbara as she stooped to put on her shoes. "If it wasn't for Mr Maber you and I would sleep in the workhouse tonight – I hope you don't snore."

Myrtle, who stood exactly four feet in height, made an oo-ing noise to express her amazement and incredulity.

"But, miss," she said in alarm, "I thought you had a bit of money of your own? I'd never have come to London – "

"London is bigger than Ilchester," Barbara broke in moodily, "which means that you meet a thousand undesirables here to every one you see in that Deadly Hole."

Myrtle shivered.

"I must say, miss, that I was surprised that you ever come up," she said. "You *do* see a bit of life in Ilchester, what with the fair and market days. I don't know a soul except the policeman – "

"If you were a modest woman you wouldn't even know the policeman," said Barbara severely; and Myrtle, nineteen next birthday and regarding London policemen as gods, went patchily red.

"Look out of the window and see if that young man has gone," said Barbara, a little inconsistently, as it appeared to the maid.

"Yes, miss" – Myrtle peered through the curtains into the gloom of Doughty Street – "no, miss."

"Make up your mind," said Barbara.

"He's there – standing at the corner. He's got a pair of grey trousis – "

"I want to know nothing about his trousers," interrupted her mistress. "Is he there?"

"Yes, miss."

"Well, blow him to blazes!" hissed Barbara.

Myrtle, undecided as to whether this was an instruction or whether it was merely an objurgation, gazed in awe at her young lady. She had always thought Barbara was lovely without exactly knowing *why* Barbara was lovely, for she was no carping analyst. She knew that Barbara had a good skin and wonderful hair, and in a vague way realised that the effect of big, grey eyes, a perfect mouth and a straight nose might have something to do with it.

But she knew complexion and hair were inseparable from the sum of perfect beauty, because she had read soap advertisements and hair advertisements, which told her intimately just what attracts young men to young women.

"Is he waiting for you, miss?" she asked, not without malice.

"Of course he's waiting for me," said Barbara icily. "You know very well that he is Mr Stewart, The Man Who Sells Space."

"Space, miss?" Myrtle was staggered. Then, remembering vaguely certain information acquired at the village school: "The sky, miss?"

"He'd sell that if you'd buy it."

Myrtle peeped again.

"Don't he know the number of the house, miss?" she asked cunningly, and Barbara gave her one look which appalled and terrified her.

She slipped on her coat, picked up her bag and umbrella, and passed out into Doughty Street as the clock was striking nine. The young man who stood against the lamp-post turned quickly at the sound of her step and lifted his hat.

"I wondered if you were – "

She silenced him with a dignified gesture.

"I don't know whether you realise the fact that you have placed me in a false position with Myrtle," she said, and talked through his apologies. "Myrtle has an aunt in Ilchester, which is my home town, and Myrtle's aunt was famous before loudspeakers were invented. Although the views of Ilchester do not disturb me in the slightest, I should like you to know that Mr Maber is a churchwarden there, and as he was responsible for bringing me to London I must protect his name."

"I am terribly sorry," said Alan Stewart penitently, "but it seems absurd to walk alone to the office when we live round the corner, so to speak."

"Couldn't you take a bus?" she asked frigidly. "Really, Mr Stewart, whilst I appreciate that you have the welfare of my employer at heart, I'd very much rather you walked to the office with him and told him so. And if your livelihood depends upon Mr Maber buying space in the newspaper you represent, or any old newspaper, you'll be sitting on the Embankment tonight gnawing your knuckles."

Mr Stewart started to protest his disinterestedness, but changed his mind.

"I have been rather a nuisance, I'm afraid. Who is Myrtle – your sister?"

"Not mine. She's somebody's, I believe. I remember seeing a whole family of large and small Myrtles."

"Your maid?" he said quickly. "I am terribly sorry."

Barbara sniffed.

"As for publicity," said Mr Alan Stewart, with the haughty indifference of one who controls the advertising revenue of three great dailies, "I've ceased to bother Mr Maber. The gentleman who thinks that having his name painted on the roof of Noah's Ark gives him sufficient publicity to last him for all eternity is no longer alive. To me he is 'the late Mr Maber.' I never pass his shop without taking off my hat and dropping a silent tear."

"Did he have his name painted on the Ark?" she asked, interested.

"It was a mere figure of speech," said Alan carelessly. "He advertises – yes. Half-page advertisements in the exclusive magazines. They are not so much advertisements as memorial notices, and what is the consequence? Whilst Maber & Maber dwindle and decay on one side of the street, the noble firm of Atterman Brothers raises its lofty head to the clouds on the other – Attermans have been established eight years; Maber & Maber have been a traffic block in the path of progress for a hundred and fifty. And that is all the business I wish to talk."

"Don't stop," she begged. "I like you in those poetical moments. When I say 'like you' " she added hastily, "I mean you are more tolerable. We don't need advertising. The name of Maber on our goods is a guarantee of purity and honest dealing."

"That would be all right if people were buying your goods," he said pointedly.

"Our place is as big as Attermans." She stopped in her walk to challenge him, a deadly frown on her face, hostility in her eyes.

"Superficially, yes. Morally, no," he said. "I like Mr Maber as a man. In point of breeding and birth he is to the Attermans as an orchid to a cauliflower."

Barbara nodded. She did not think it was necessary to tell him that Mr Maber was her god-father, and he never knew that she had bullied him into bringing her to London, or that when he had, with the greatest reluctance, put her in his office as his private secretary, she had, by sheer capability, made herself indispensable.

"As to Mr Julius Colesberg, the junior partner of your moribund business, he is about as much use to Mr Maber as a cooking-stove in – well, any hot place you can think of."

Here again she reluctantly agreed with him. She looked round at him: straight-backed, broad-shouldered.

"Why are you an advertising man?" she asked bluntly. "You look more like a soldier."

"I was an advertising man before I was a soldier," he said diplomatically, "and one must live."

"Why?" asked Barbara.

"I suppose there is no reason why one shouldn't live – " he began.

"No, I don't mean that," she interrupted. "Haven't you heard the call of the great open spaces that comes to all young heroes?"

"The only open spaces that interest me – " he began.

"Don't let us talk shop," she begged. "Have you heard of the wide lands under God's sky where men are men?"

He nodded bravely.

"Not only heard, but read," he said. "I've just sold three half-pages to the Western Albert Development Company. And, anyway, I see as many films as you – and I couldn't very well miss that wide lands stuff. By the way" – his voice was serious now – "Atterman had a conference with Mr Maber this morning."

"How do you know?" she asked in surprise.

"I know everything. You can't keep things from Fleet Street."

"Where is that?" she asked, and he could afford to smile.

He left her at the corner of Marlborough Avenue and she went on alone, past the sedate windows of Maber & Maber, with their exquisite materials, so pretty to see, so difficult to sell, and she stopped at the big swing-doors and looked across at the glaring white façade of Attermans, five stories high and bristling with flags, to advertise the fact that, no matter what was your nationality, Mr Atterman and his staff would be glad to take your money.

Three men were busy in one of the store windows, preparing a new display. Attermans frequently figured as defendants in the police court, charged with obstruction, for their window shows invariably collected crowds which made the sidewalk impassable. Almost every other bus that passed by bore the magic legend, "Attermans means Happy Shopping."

"Curse them!" said Barbara cold-bloodedly, passing through the doors.

She went up to the office, observed by the scowling Mr Lark, who held the dual position of chief buyer and accountant – an amazing circumstance: he buys best who knows not the shallowness of the purse. And just now Mabers' official coffers sounded rather hollow.

Mr Lark paused in his work as Barbara came in, and his pale eyes surveyed her malignantly.

"Ten minutes late," he said tremulously. "If I had my way I'd take that girl and put her straight into the street! I'd say to her, 'Miss Barbara Storr, here's your money – beat it! I don't want you round this office giving yourself almighty airs. Go and find another job.' I would, indeed!"

The audience, his stenographer, made a clicking noise which expressed both her sympathy and her awe at the latent strength of the man.

"I'd no more think of saying 'you're fired' than I'd think of – of anything," the gaunt accountant went on. "What's a private secretary but a menial? A sort of domestic servant, like my housemaid. That's what she is – a menial! Runs and carries for Tom, Dick and Harry."

"It's dreadful," agreed his typist vaguely.

"Dreadful?" snarled the gentleman to whom Barbara Storr invariably referred as "Hark, hark, the Lark." "Why, she treats even Mr Julius like a dog! She does! Treats him like a dog! A partner! Socialism's the ruin of the age."

"Is she a Socialist?" asked Miss Leverby, interested.

"I know nothing about her," said the accountant and buyer testily. "Those kind of people I don't meet – socially. If I saw her in the street

I wouldn't so much as raise my hat to her. I'm vindictive. When anybody gets in wrong with me I just give 'em – hell!"

Miss Leverby shivered appropriately at the great word.

"She's always going on about advertising – one of the lowest things that ever came into business. Nags Mr Maber! I've heard her. And then she wants to know why we don't stock this, that and the other. I says to her the other day 'Miss S.,' I says, 'if people don't like what we sell they can go somewhere else.' 'They do,' she says. 'Look at Attermans – you can buy anything there from a pie to a pistol' – those were her very words. I says to her, '*Miss* S. – this is a quality house – we've been established a hundred and fifty years. Everybody knows us – we don't have to do anything vulgar, or sell anything shoddy.' 'You have to,' she says, 'but you don't know how to,' she says. My Gawd! These people go on as if they *owned* the place."

"T-t!" said the audience, shocked.

"That girl's got some hold over Maber," concluded Mr Lark darkly. "Mark my words. There was a case like it in the Sunday newspapers. You may have seen the headline – 'Young girl holds Aged Millionaire in a Grip of Iron.' That's her!"

It was part of the cussedness of things that Barbara's covert antagonism to the junior partner should come to a head that morning.

His secretary was away with a cold, and Barbara went in to take down a letter. She disliked Julius instinctively. He was a suave, young-looking man in the thirties, sallow of face and somewhat perfumed. Barbara loathed men who used scent and wore diamond rings, but never, until that morning, had the dislike taken active shape.

"Morning, Miss Storr." He looked up from the Empire desk where he was sorting over his letters. "Old man here?"

"Mr Maber hasn't arrived yet," she said.

Julius unfolded an exquisite cambric handkerchief and wiped his lips thoughtfully.

"That conference is coming on today," he said. "Attermans are making a – very – fair – offer. Mr Maber is getting old – I think he'd be foolish not to take a price."

Julius had come straight from Atterman's house in Regent's Park that morning. They had breakfasted together and certain agreements had been reached. Such things are done. Mr Colesberg had a one-twenty-fifth share in the business and no active management. A sale at Atterman's figure would give him a large holding and the direction. Such things happen.

Barbara opened her notebook and poised her pencil suggestively.

"Now listen, child." Julius in a fatherly mood made her feel a little faint. "You'll be at the conference and you'll be doing yourself and everybody a good turn if you use your undoubted influence."

"Toward what?"

"The sale. The business is going down; it wants activity, it wants advertising – it wants everything that an old-fashioned man won't give it."

Her lips curled offensively.

"Is this the man who told Mr Maber that advertising would vulgarise Mabers" she demanded.

"In the circumstances I was right," he said hastily. "Mabers couldn't do it – Attermans could. Do you see what I mean, little girl?"

"Don't call me 'little girl' – it makes me feel old," she said. "And when Atterman takes charge of this place, will he start a Ladies' Lusiana Orchestra?"

An innocent and seemingly pointless remark, but for the affair of the beautiful blonde solo player. In justice to the man with whom he had breakfasted, Julius uttered a grave protest.

"The jury gave a verdict to Atterman," he said, "And, anyway, she should have been ashamed of herself to bring an action for breach of promise against a man like Mr Atterman – a magnate!"

"Maudie loved him," said Barbara outrageously, "She lives near me – I often walk home with her. She's so upset she can't play anything but hymns."

"I wonder she plays at all," said Julius primly. "It is very unwomanly to play on the cornet."

"She'll be playing on the harp soon unless something happens," said Barbara ominously. "Now what about these letters?"

She had taken down two of his epistles and she was waiting for the third, when, absent-mindedly, he laid his long and bony hand on hers. Barbara got up slowly.

"Is that all, Mr Colesberg?"

"That is all," he said, and then, as he walked to the door and stood aside to let her go out of the room, he murmured something about "a little bit of dinner and a show."

"Is this invitation from Mrs Colesberg?" she asked.

"Not married," said Julius, nibbling at his nails. "Can't stand marriage. You know what I mean...being tied up to some woman... positively dreadful. I'll meet you at the corner of Haymarket. Make it eight – I don't like to rush my dressing. And wear something quiet...see what I mean? A girl looks best in black. If she starts to wear colours she gets conspicuous and makes a fellow noticed..."

"Which end of the Haymarket?" asked Barbara.

"Top end – corner of Jermyn Street. You'll recognise me – "

"I might possibly mistake you for a wireworm," interrupted Barbara gently. "I think you had better have your name in electric lights – round your hat! Or perhaps if you carried a banner – blue is my favourite colour – or came in a pink golfing suit. I should hate to miss you."

Colesberg's sallow face turned a dark crimson.

"You've a nerve to talk to me like that!" he spluttered. "You – you – if I've any authority in the place I'll have you out of this office today! You give yourself the airs of a duchess and go on as if you... I'll not stand it! I'll – I'll see Maber as soon as he arrives..."

"I'll ring you just the minute he comes in," said Barbara with great politeness.

She was hardly in her room before Mr Maber's bell rang and, gathering up her notebook and pencil, she opened the door and went in.

Mr Maber was a large man both up and down and backwards and forwards. It was difficult to believe that he had ever rowed six except in a lifeboat, which is built to stand almost any kind of strain. Yet as a

brawny youth he had occupied that position in the Cambridge eight
– the year they beat Oxford so unexpectedly.

He called himself old-fashioned when he was really lethargic; he
abhorred modern tendencies in business and sugariness in church
music. He was a churchwarden of St Asaph's, Ilchester, and took his
duties seriously.

His life, he was apt to say, sometimes proudly, sometimes regretfully,
was an open book. If there were two pages that were scientifically
gummed together, the deliquency thus concealed was a fairly little
one. It had to do with a dinner given to the combined crews on Boat
Race night. It was the Saturday before Marcus Elbury, the stroke and
his school friend, went to the United States; and after the dinner he
and Marcus had paid a visit to the Empire Theatre. They went in at
nine-forty-five singing a cheery song – in those days it was a music-
hall and a song was not out of place. At nine-fifty they came out,
accompanied by four commissionaires, three policemen and a cloak-
room attendant. At this point of the story a lady came into it; but
the open book was gummed very securely. He simply refused to think
of what followed. If he thought at all, it was as a man thinks of his end:
momentarily, and then a scramble of mind to get to something more
pleasant.

Mr Maber had found himself musing on those strange days. He had
been a comfortably situated young man and could well afford to pay
forty shillings and to compensate the policemen both for their torn
tunics and certain transitory damage to their features. The sequel he
could not afford…however, he never thought of that.

And Marcus was coming back for Saturday's dinner. Mr Maber was
entertaining the Cambridge eight; he wondered whether this 1911
wine was as good as people said it was.

Now and again, as he came nearer to Marlborough Avenue, a
thought of business intruded into his pleasing meditations, and he
shuddered. He would be glad to have done with it all; the vulgar
proximity of Attermans alone was sufficient to sicken him. In a vague
way he wished he could keep abreast of the times and maintain in
flower the seedling five generations of Mabers had tended. Mr Maber

sighed. He was a rich man, but somehow he could never bring himself to selling out real securities and reinvesting in Mabers.

He came gloomily to his office, hung up his hat and umbrella and allowed Barbara to help him out of his coat.

"Well, Barbara," he said glumly, "we shall soon be out of this — back in Ilchester. No place like it, Barbara."

He shook his head sorrowfully. The thought did not seem to arouse any hilarious sense of happiness.

"You won't stay, of course," he said. "We'll find a job for you at Knapp House. What would you like to be?"

"If I'm going back to Ilchester I should rather like to be dead," she said calmly.

He was mildly shocked.

"It is a great old town," he said in a hushed voice, as though he feared that Ilchester might overhear him and get all puffed up; "a grand old town. That dear old carillon from the Minster!"

"And those dear old mosquitoes that breed in the horse-pond," she said; "and those dear old ladies who have nothing to do but tell you why people marry in a hurry!"

"Barbara!" He murmured. He was (he remembered at odd moments) a churchwarden.

She gave him his letters and he glanced at them.

"What time is the conference?" he asked.

"In twenty minutes."

He pinched his lip.

"We had better have Lark up; he knows the business. And Mr Colesberg, of course. Atterman is bringing his general manager."

"Monkey?" said Barbara.

"Minkey, I think," said her employer gravely, and sighed.

"Mr Maber, why are you selling this business?" she asked. "I'm sure there is a tremendous fortune in it — if it was properly run. What is the use of men like Lark? I don't want him to lose his job; he ought to get a rise of ten per cent, on condition he kept away from the office. Buyer! I wouldn't trust him to buy a mouse-trap!"

"We do not sell mouse-traps," said Mr Maber.

"Why don't you sell what people want, when you find that they don't want what you sell? If I had this business" – she was glaring at him – "I'd put Attaboy in his place. And you could! Every line he sells we've had on offer. He puts money into advertisements and gets it back over the counter…"

She paused, out of breath. Mr Maber was regarding her with admiration and pity.

"I am too old to change round," he said pathetically, and in the same breath: "Get the Trocadero, my dear, and ask them to put a few – er – crackers on the table – something with caps inside…these boys like that kind of foolery – and – er – tell them that I want magnums, not quarts…these youngsters after months of training are not satisfied with quarts – um…"

He thought of Marcus and smiled whimsically. That night…who hit the road first, he or Marcus? For thirty years they had disputed the matter by letter.

"And now, my dear, go along and see if those people are in the board-room. Be sure Mr Atterman is made comfortable."

A condemned man might, in the same tone and with equal sincerity, have sent to ask if the hangman had slept well.

Mr Atterman was thin, loose-jointed and lightly dressed. He wore horn-rimmed glasses and was anxious to be mistaken for an American. To this end he cultivated idiomatics from the comic supplements of the New York Sunday newspapers. In point of fact he came from the opposite direction.

"Why, I'm real glad to see you, Mr Maber – meet Mr Hercules Minkey."

Mr Minkey was small, round-shouldered, flat-faced. His nose was broad and short, his dark eyes were small and deep. The influence of names upon physical and mental growth is a subject for psychological examination. In all the circumstances his name was unfortunate. But he was what Mr Atterman would and did call a live wire. Which is another name for a man who disagrees with everybody and finds another way of doing things wrong.

"Glad to meet you, Miss Storr. My! I envy you your secretary, Mr Maber. That's the one Storr I'd like to buy with *your* store! Ha, ha! I hope we'll be able to persuade you to stay along right here, Miss Storr."

Julius was there, eating the end of a pen absent-mindedly. Mr Lark came a little importantly, smirked at Mr Atterman, bowed to Mr Maber, nodded familiarly to Mr Minkey, smiled respectfully at Julius, and took no notice of Barbara.

"Now we're all here together," said Mr Atterman. "I'll lay my proposition right down in front of you. Don't make a note of this, Miss Storr. I'll tell you where the proceedings start. As I say, we've got together…"

Barbara was to start at that part of the speech where the price was mentioned. When at last the sum was stated, she was paralysed. She looked at Mr Maber. He sat with clasped hands and pursed lips, unmoved.

"A hundred thousand pounds!" she was exasperated in exclaiming. "Why, the freehold is worth nearly that – "

Mr Atterman looked hard at her. For the moment she was not the kind of store that he would like to have bought. Julius was glowering; Mr Lark was almost articulate in his indignation.

"If you'll allow me, young lady, we'll get right along," said Mr Atterman deliberately.

He got right along. Mr Maber closed his eyes. The Lark closed his eyes too; probably the last act of loyalty to his employer.

"The offer is very small – very small indeed," murmured Mr Maber, when his rival had got where he was getting.

Mr Atterman drew a long breath, put his head on one side and, looking at the table, raised his eyebrows. It meant that he was sorry.

"I thought personally – " Mr Maber looked at Barbara.

"Half a million," said Barbara.

"Really, Maber!" Julius threw the uneaten portion of his pen upon the table.

Mr Lark was making horrified noises.

13

"Perhaps you had better – um – content yourself with taking a record," said Mr Maber, addressing the girl; and then, with great spirit: "Miss Storr is my confidential secretary – please remember that."

He looked round a little fearfully as though he expected somebody would assault him for his audacity. Everybody he saw was shrugging except Barbara and Mr Lark. Mr Lark would have shrugged, only he didn't see that the other people were doing it, and by the time he started shrugging the rest of the company (except Barbara and Mr Maber) were smiling tolerantly. They were difficult people to keep up with.

"See here, Mr Maber, if I may be allowed to speak."

The Live Wire turned himself sideways to the table. He was not American either; he took his idioms at fourth hand from Mr Atterman, and they weren't quite so natural.

"This business of yours – you don't mind me speaking frankly? – is punk – "

"How do you spell it?" interrupted Barbara coldly.

The Live Wire sparked viciously in her direction.

"Your business is punk, and for why? Because to turn this proposition into a profit-making – er – "

"Proposition," suggested Barbara.

"You gotta spend a hundred thousand pounds *more*. Now take our store…"

He took his store and analysed it in all its aspects and bearings. Barbara closed her eyes and dozed. He had that kind of voice. Some divines have it. There are people to whom veronal is an irritant and morphia a pick-me-up, who can lay their heads against the knobby corner of a pew with a smile almost before the text is thoroughly established. Odd scraps of information – strange technicalities – intruded into her dreams.

"Now take overhead charges…well, I figure it out that an intensive publicity campaign… Every knock's a boost…"

"Barbara."

She came to life as Mr Atterman was saying "good-bye."

"Well, it hasn't got to the lawyer stage, but I think we've made progress. I'm not going to kick over twenty thousand one way or the other."

As he left the board-room he caught the eye of Mr Julius Colesberg, and that gentleman followed him into the corridor.

"Who is this fresh kid, Julius?" he asked wrathfully. "Get on to the old man, for the love of Mike, and tip him off that I'm not the sort of guy to stand for a fresh stenographer butting into my business."

"Sure," said Julius, infected.

"I'll go up to a hundred and twenty thousand. Stock at valuation; and the goodwill is worth about ten cents. I'll have the contract ready on Monday -- fix the meeting and bring along your lawyer."

He gave Julius a cigar, and Julius, who did not smoke cigars, tried to look pleased.

"It's a Claro, too," he said in sycophantic awe. "My favourite breed!"

Almost immediately after the meeting Mr Maber went out to lunch. He went hurriedly, guiltily, and did not meet Barbara's eye. Her heart went down; he was going to sell. And when, after he came back from lunch, he deposited the massive catalogue of Messrs Carper & Suthern, the eminent seed specialists, on his desk, and talked about laying out a new rose garden, she groaned.

"The truth is, Barbara, I want quiet and peace. Why should I bother with business? I have an enormous lot of money – in fact, I have so much that I intend dividing half the sum I receive from this sale amongst the employees of Maber & Maber. Why *should* I slave and fret in a business which is wholly uncongenial? What do I know of ladies' outfitting? What interest have I in cami – well, whatever we sell? Why should I grow agitated with the fluctuations of foulard and the gyrations of georgette? It is a wholly indelicate occupation for a man who is – er – an old blue, and whose tendencies are towards the study of ecclesiastical law. By the way, Barbara, you might ring up the Trocadero and tell them that I wish nothing but light blue flowers for table decorations tomorrow night. Would you like to see the boat race, Barbara? I can find you a place on the Leander launch, and I'd like you to meet my old friend Marcus: we were at Cambridge together in eighty-four. That's a long time ago."

"Would nothing induce you to keep this business in your hands?" she asked desperately.

Mr Maber looked dubious.

"We show an increasing loss. Julius Colesberg is a young man full of fire and energy, yet he can do nothing. New blood, my dear – that is what we require."

He sighed heavily.

"Julius Colesberg!"

Mr Maber shifted uncomfortably. He did not like his partner, but had admitted him to a share in the business on very favourable terms because he entertained the secret hope that Julius would supply the energy and enthusiasm which he, as an older man, lacked. Julius was to be the live wire (Mr Maber, who had no idea that wires could live, referred to him as an "energising factor"). As a driving force, Julius was not a conspicuous success. He had cast his bread upon the waters of Maber & Maber in the confident belief that it would return in the form of buttered toast. He was ornamental to a point; his manicurist told him that he had the most beautiful hands she had ever seen. Almost every man she told this was pleased; Julius purred.

"Well…I'll be better out of it. The stress of competition, the vulgar pushing and bawling in the market-place, the hustle and bustle of it all, are distasteful to me, Barbara."

He went home early, and Barbara, miserable at heart, loafed round the departments. The news of the impending sale had flashed from the laces to the silks, from the ribbons to the stockings; young goddesses in black saw her wandering disconsolately and arched their pencilled eyebrows. Floor-walkers in immaculate frock-coats were guardedly polilte, knowing something of the feud that existed between the Colesberg-Lark section and the lady who was popularly supposed to dominate the boss; for how did they know that too great effusiveness on their part might not lead to their undoing if the boss went? At the same time, an attitude leaning towards silliness might as easily bring them to destruction if the sale fell through.

"Never in my life," said Mr Lark, giving a brief but flattering description of the part he played at the conference, "have I seen such nerve! What was she? A mere shorthand-writer, taking down the words and notions, so to speak, of keen business men."

"And she put her spoke in?" said the stenopgraher in an awe-stricken voice.

Mr Lark closed his eyes and nodded.

"I stopped her right away," he said. "I turned to her and just gave her one look. And then I said, quietly and politely, 'Keep your place, Storr.' I may have said 'Miss Storr' – I'm not certain. Well" – he leant back in his chair and rubbed his hands – "we're not going to see much more of *that* young lady."

"When is she going, Mr Lark?" asked the stenographer, with visions of advancement.

"On Tuesday. We take over on Monday."

The Lark had already agreed with Julius, in a confidential interview, to separate his occupations and remain head accountant at an increased salary.

"And on Tuesday, if she's got the nerve to come, I shall be waiting on the doorstep. 'Excuse me, Miss Storr,' I shall say, 'where are you going?' 'Up to my office, Mr Lark,' she'll say. 'Oh, no, indeed,' I'll say, 'you don't come here, and if you give me any trouble I shall send for the police.' "

"Ooh!" said his typist, impressed.

Mr Maber seldom came to the office on Saturdays. On this the day of all days in the year, his appearance in a place of business could only be due to mental aberration. He was, in fact, sitting in the bow of a river steamer with another stout man, similarly well wrapped, and for fifteen hectic minutes he was standing up, red in the face, telling the Cambridge stroke what to do. There were some fifty thousand others giving advice more or less similar. They lined the river-banks, they crowded on barges, they ventured perilously in dinghies, and yelled and roared as the two lean eights swung across the finishing line with Cambridge half a boat in front...

At ten o'clock that night Mr Maber leant across the glittering table and said to the strong-featured man seated next to the Cambridge captain:

"Marcus, do you remember that night at the Empire?"

"Shall I ever forget it?" said Marcus with a happy sigh.

"Do you remember what we did to the youthful commissionaire who threw me down the first flight of steps?"

"The man you wanted to fight?" asked Marcus. "I haven't a very clear recollection of the circumstances, but I have a dim idea that it was the second flight down which you were thrown."

"The first flight," said Mr Maber firmly. "I distinctly remember there was a mat at the bottom."

Mr Maber leant back in his chair, pursed his lips and held his long glass of port to the light before he drank it slowly. It seemed to taste better than the first glass; if anything, was more exquisite of bouquet than the seventh.

"I wonder if he's still alive?" he mused. "He was a comparatively young man. I remember he had a mole on his nose."

"Let's go and see," said Marcus, rising slowly from the table; for the dinner was over and the party had already dwindled to the captain of the Cambridge crew, a polite man who was spoiling a glorious evening through an excess of good manners.

"Yes, we will go and see." Mr Maber rose too. "I feel that I should like to tell him – the mole-nosed man – that he was grossly insolent. It is curious" – he shook his head in wonder – "that all these years it has never occurred to me to call at the Empire Theatre and tell him what I think of him."

"By the way," said Marcus Elbury, stopping, "what happened to Her?" He saw the pain in his friend's face. "Sorry," he said penitently. "Let's go find that fresh feller with the mole."

The conference was fixed for twelve o'clock on Monday. Barbara was not aware of the fact until she got to the office and found a memorandum on Mr Maber's desk to this effect. It was the first visible evidence of the coming of the new authority. Mr Maber had not arrived at ten; at eleven he was still absent, but this was not unusual. At a quarter past eleven an office boy came in a state of agitation and said that a policeman wished to speak to her.

"A policeman, Tommy? Tell him to come in."

The officer arrived – a tall, saturnine man, who closed the door behind him.

"Are you Miss Storr?" he asked.

She nodded, inwardly quaking.

"Miss Barbara Storr?"

"Yes, that is my name."

"Will you come along to Marlborough Street, miss?" he asked in a hoarse whisper. "Nobody knows except me and the inspector."

Her jaw dropped.

"The police station?"

"The court," he corrected. "Don't think hard of him – he's a very nice gentleman, and the reporters say they'll keep his name out of the papers – though nobody knows who he is... Mind you, miss, the magistrate wasn't vindictive. You can't go biting people's ears, not even on a Boat Race night, without arousing, so to speak, animosity. And a month's hard labour without the option – "

"A month?" she gasped. "Who has got a month?"

He looked round.

"Mr Maber," he said, and she clutched at the edge of the table for support.

"But – but – " she stammered. She found her voice at last. "Surely they can fine him?"

The policeman shook his head.

"No, miss. You come along – he wants to see you before they take him to Pentonville. I'll go first so as not to create any suspicion, and you follow."

A quarter of an hour later a dazed Barbara passed into the inspector's office at Marlborough Street and was welcomed with the geniality which the police display towards all law-abiding ladies.

"He's in the cells with a lawyer just now," said the inspector, "but I think you can go in."

He led her across the wide hall, crowded with the troubled friends of the ladies and gentlemen who soon were to appear at the bar of judgment, and through a door along the passage.

"Wait here," said the inspector, and, passing through another door, returned in a few minutes and beckoned her.

They were in a corridor along one side of which ran a number of small, terrifying doors; she noted this before she saw Mr Maber. He was in slightly soiled evening dress, minus tie and collar, and he was unshaven. Beneath his right eye was a large dark blue discolouration, and he would have smiled with difficulty owing to a swelling of the upper lip. However, he showed no disposition to smile.

"Barbara," he said in a hushed voice, "I want you to do something for me. This is Mr Hammett, a lawyer."

It was not his own lawyer, she knew, and guessed that it was help he had acquired locally.

"This is dreadful, and it all happened because the man refused to come outside and fight like a gentleman. It is absurd to say that I bit him…it must have been a dog. I saw one – in fact several."

His speech was a little wild and incoherent. She understood his agitation and sympathised with him.

His speech was a little wild and incoherent. She understood his agitation and sympathised with him.

"I'll be away a month," he said. "There were not reporters in court, and I didn't give my right address," he added, with fierce pleasure; and that was the only satisfaction he seemed to have got out of the business. "Tell the people at the office that I've been called abroad. Have you got that paper?" He turned to the lawyer, who handed him a foolscap form bearing two tiny red seals.

"The commissioner will be here in a minute," said the lawyer, and almost as he spoke the door swung open and a tall man with a heavy moustache appeared. "Here he is."

The commissioner took a tiny book from his waistcoat pocket, said something very rapidly, and Mr Maber signed a paper he held with the lawyer's fountain pen.

"Barbara, you've got to look after things. You're the only person I can trust. As to the sale…get the best terms you can…"

"What is this?"

"That is a power of attorney," said Mr Maber urgently. "Somebody must look after the – er – office whilst I am away. There are cheques to sign, and I simply dare not let anybody know of this disgrace." He thought of Ilchester and groaned.

Barbara took the paper like a little girl in a dream.

"What does this mean?"

"It means you do everything in my name," he said. "I'm sure I can trust you, Barbara."

"Sign cheques?" she asked.

"Sign anything," said Mr Maber, a little impatiently. "There's nobody else in the world to whom I can give so wide a power. But it's necessary, Barbara. Tell them I have gone to Cannes or Monte Carlo."

"I shall tell them Cologne," said Barbara gently. "We had better make it a cathedral city."

2

Barbara came through the door leading to the cells, clutching a white paper in her hand, and with the last words of Mr Maber ringing through her mind.

"Give him ten pounds – I haven't any money."

Dimly she realised that the "him" referred to was the little lawyer by her side. He was a thin and tiny man; his clothes were shabby and rusty; his collar had been left over from last week's wash; and obviously he had not met a razor, except socially, for days and days. Hollow-eyed, hollow-cheeked, he smiled up at her.

"You won't want me to send you a bill, Miss Storr?" he said, and murmured something about "keeping his books clear." "Jolly old boy!" he said enthusiastically as she groped in her bag. "You can't be old if your heart's young. Married, miss?"

"I? Certainly not!"

"Not you, miss – old cherry-face – what a lad!"

"Mr Maber is a bachelor, so far as I know," said Barbara, more intent upon finding the money than Mr Maber's blessed state.

She had more than sufficient money in her bag. She was paid well, and it was the beginning of the week.

"Ten pounds?"

"Guineas," said Mr Hammett rather sadly.

He took the money and slipped it into his trousers pocket with a sidelong glance at the door.

"Any little service I can render you, Miss Storr, will you be kind enough to communicate with me?"

He handed her a dingy card, and glancing at it she saw, to her surprise, that the address was Lambeth. The phone number had been scratched out.

"Temporarily out of order," he said airily, following her eyes. "These telephones are always going wrong."

Barbara, who knew that telephones went wrong easiest when the quarterly fees were not promptly settled, gave him a smile and a handshake. With a flourish of his silk hat he made for the street. A young man who had been evidently waiting for him stepped up as he came abreast.

"Excuse me, Mr Hammett," he said. "You *are* Mr Hammett?"

"That is my name, boy," said Hammett, a little haughtily.

"Sorry," said the youth, and passed him a folded blue paper.

Mr Hammett raised his eyebrows, glanced at the superscription and thrust the offending document into his pocket.

"You can tell your principal that this matter will be settled today," he said with great severity.

The inspector was standing at the door of his room, a beaming spectator of the comedy.

"Come inside, miss," he said. "I'm sorry your governor got Hammett, but I suppose he did all he wanted."

"Who is he?" asked Barbara, who was now in a new world.

"He's a solicitor, I suppose," said the inspector. "At any rate, he's never been struck off the rolls. One of the old snide lawyers that tout the South London police court. We always get him up here after Boat Race night, and as a rule he's picked up a client or two. I'm sorry about Mr Maber," he went on in a more serious tone. "I know him well. He's been very good to my old mother, who lives in Ilchester. You come from there, miss, don't you? I've seen you there time and time again."

"Yes," said the girl in surprise, and then: "Did he really bite anybody?"

"Mr Maber? I don't know; they say he did," said the inspector. "But, Lord bless your life! What's a bite? May have been done playfully."

23

The tall, cadaverous constable who had come for her was standing in the inspector's room. He was evidently employed on messenger duty.

"I wonder you don't have a couple of policemen down at your place, miss," said the inspector. "Attermans have got them. They've three or four."

"Can you employ policemen?" she asked, open-eyed.

The inspector laughed.

"Why, yes, miss, with permission from the Commissioner. You have to pay for them, of course, but a big store can generally have as many as they want at sale time."

To think, with Barbara, was to act.

"I'll buy one," she said. "How much do they cost?"

"You can't buy one outright, miss," said the staggered inspector. "You can hire them. I'll put through an enquiry if you wish. Have you any particular man you'd like?"

She pointed to the tall, cadaverous constable.

"I'll have that one."

The inspector scratched his chin.

"I dare say it can be arranged, miss. Outside or inside duty?"

"Inside," said Barbara promptly.

It was an idea.

She called a taxicab and drove to Mr Maber's bank, interviewed a dumbfounded manager, produced a specimen of her signature, and was entering her cab again when a voice hailed her. She turned round to meet a fair girl with large, expressive eyes and lips which were even redder than the rose.

"Fancy meeting you, Miss Storr!" Maudie Deane grasped her hand warmly. "I've just been up to try to see Atterman. You'd think that, being a gentleman, and having, so to speak, spoilt all my chances – "

"Come into the cab. I'm in a hurry."

The solo cornetist in the Lusiana Ladies' Orchestra followed her into the taxi.

"Now, Maudie," said Barbara, "tell me about it all over again. I have a special reason for wishing to know everything that I can know about Atterman. He did fall in love with you – he did promise to marry you?"

Maudie nodded, her blue eyes filled with tears.

"I started the band for Atterman," she said. "It was my idea. I've played the cornet since I was six. My dear dad was the greatest soloist that this world has ever known – or any other world," she added. "And naturally Mr Atterman took to me. I'm a lady, whatever else I am. He used to come down every lunch-time and stand just where he could see me, his eyes, so to speak, devouring me, if I may use a romantic expression. It got so on my mind that I used to play flat. I think he wanted to marry me, but his mother – "

Barbara gasped.

"His mother? Has a man like that got a mother?"

"He's got two," was the astounding reply – "a stepmother and a real mother. His papa was divorced in sad circumstances. It appears – "

"I don't want to know anything about the sad circumstances," said Barbara hastily. "Go on with your love lyric."

The girl cast a pained look at her companion.

"It started with his seeing me home and holding hands…you know. He's an honourable man; I will say that for him. But both the mothers took a violent dislike to me."

"Both of them? Did you meet them both?"

Maudie nodded.

"Only one of them talks English, but I could tell by the other one's looks – Mr Atterman was originally a Russian gentleman. They took a violent dislike to me. I'd never have brought him into court, only my papa said that my honour should be vindicated, and that I was certain to get a good music-hall engagement with all the publicity – which I haven't. Miss Storr," she gulped, "I love that man!"

Barbara could only look at her in wonder.

"I suppose you'll see a lot of him now?" sobbed Maudie, dabbing her eyes. "You lucky girl!"

"Seeing Mr Atterman is not exactly my idea of a windfall," said Barbara carefully; "but why should I be seeing a lot of him?"

25

Maudie dried her eyes with a tiny handkerchief in which was harboured a small, round, woolly object that imparted an immediate pallor to her red nose.

"They're buying your business. I met Mr Minkey on the street and he told me. He's certainly a live wire, that man – and musical! I taught him his notes; he plays the concertina divinely. He says they're going to make a provision department of Attermans in your store. Percy Atterman is certainly a wonderful man!"

Barbara left the sometime soloist of the Lusiana Ladies' Orchestra gazing raptly across the road at the shell which had once held her ambitions. Barbara hurried through the store, up the narrow stairs to the office. As she passed Mr Lark's office he called to her.

"Storr!"

She turned back.

"What time is Mr Maber coming?"

"Lark, I can't tell you," she replied.

"I've got a handle to my name," he said loudly, conscious that his appreciative staff were listening.

Barbara looked at him thoughtfully for a long time, and then:

"I won't fire you, because I know that you are married and your wife has enough trouble. But your appointment as chief buyer in the firm of Maber & Maber terminates today. I will let you have it in writing."

Mr Lark was speechless; could remember no retort until she was back in her office.

She threw her coat and hat on a chair, stalked into Mr Maber's private room, sat down, looked through his letters, threw them aside, called Mr Stewart on the telephone, and then rang the bell. Mr Lark, thinking mistakenly that his employer had returned, hurried to lay his complaint before him; for this was a moment when he could afford to speak his mind.

He nearly dropped at the sight of the girl in the chair.

"Come in, Lark, and sit down." She pointed to a chair.

"See here, Miss Storr – " he began.

She raised her hand.

"What time is the conference?" she asked.

"It's waiting now," he said loudly.

"Very good," said Barbara.

She took up a pencil, stuck it in her hair and walked out of the room, and Mr Lark came behind her at a respectful distance, for it occurred to him that conceit, vanity, bumptiousness and those other attributes with which she was credited had turned the head of Miss Barbara Storr.

She opened the door of the board-room and walked in. Julius was in earnest confabulation with Mr Atterman and Minkey, and all seemed rather pleased with themselves. Two men, one of whom she saw was a stranger, and guessed was a lawyer, were comparing drafts near the chairman's end of the table. Mr Maber's grey-haired lawyer gave her a nod and a smile, which faded as she seated herself in the president's padded chair. The crime was also witnessed from the doorway by Mr Lark, who tiptoed in, lest any untoward noise should put out of the head of Mr Julius the unpleasant sentiments which, from all symptoms, he was about to deliver.

"Where is Mr Maber?" he asked sharply.

"He won't be able to come." There was a little book on the table, where the directors signed their names. Barbara dipped her pen into the ink and wrote "Barbara Storr" in large firm characters.

"Then I'll take the chair," said Julius.

He approached that sacred piece of furniture and waited. Barbara did not even look up.

"Come, come, miss," snapped Atterman sharply. "We can't wait all day, and I'm not so sure that we shall require your presence."

"I'm not so sure that I shall require yours, Mr Atterman." She leaned back in the chair, the tips of her fingers touching, in the manner immortalised by the sleuth of Baker Street.

Mr Lark looked from one to the other, turning his head so rapidly that any uninformed observer might have imagined that he was denying his responsibility for the amazing behaviour of one who was practically a subordinate. Maber's lawyer tried to pour oil on the troubled waters.

"Come, come, Miss Storr," he said good-humouredly. "I'm afraid you'll have to vacate the chair. Have you any message from Mr Maber?"

"Yes," said Barbara.

She took the power of attorney from her bag, unfolded it and passed it across to the lawyer.

"That is his message, Mr Steele."

The solicitor fixed his glasses and read from "Know all men by these presents" to "Signed before me, a Commissioner of Oaths." He was too old a lawyer, his experience too wide, to be surprised at anything. He finished reading the document and folded it up.

"Would you like me to keep this?" he said.

"I think I would, Mr Steele," said the girl. She had been wondering what she should do with the paper, and his suggestion was a relief.

"What is it all about?" demanded Julius, red in the face with annoyance.

"Do you wish to take the chair and conduct these negotiations?"

Steele was addressing the girl, and Barbara nodded.

"She conduct the negotiations? What on earth possesses you?" demanded Julius savagely. "This girl is a clerk, a stenographer, a typist – anything you like."

Mr Steele leant back and polished his glasses with a little smile. He did not like Julius.

"That's just what she is – anything she likes," he said. "And I'm afraid, gentlemen, that much as you dislike the situation, as you evidently do, Miss Barbara Storr is in control of this business."

Julius sat down hurriedly on Mr Minkey's knee and was immediately hoisted to his feet again.

"Are you mad?" he asked hollowly. "In charge of this business!... Where do I come in?"

"You come in as a junior partner, Mr Colesberg," said Steele; "and if I remember your contract, you are precluded from interfering with the operations of the senior partner or his nominee. This young lady holds Mr Maber's full power of attorney."

A deadly silence fell upon the meeting. Mr Lark's mouth opened wider and wider. Then it was true! "Young Girl Holds Millionarie in Grip of Iron"! Mr Atterman, an opportunist, was the first to recover.

"Well, now, isn't this a remarkable situation?" he said. "I'm going to tell you right here and now, ladies and gentlemen, that I'm just as ready to negotiate with Miss Storr as I am with Mr Maber. And readier," he added. "We've got in this young lady a keen business intellect, a brain outside the ordinary, though perhaps not as experienced as some of us in the art of management and finance. And personally I'm glad to know that her signature will be at the foot of this historic document."

Julius walked dully to his seat at the far end of the table, and now sat with clasped hands, watching her in a dazed and helpless fashion.

"Where do I come in?" he squeaked again, but Mr Atterman silenced him with a look.

Mr Minkey took his cue from his master.

"This proposition which we're putting forward, Miss Storr," he said briskly, his small eyes blinking at every syllable, "is – "

"Where is Maber?" Julius was goaded into asking the question.

"He's abroad," said Barbara. "In Germany."

"Where? I'm not going to be quiet, Atterman – I want to know. Where is Mr Maber? What part of Germany."

Barbara missed Cologne, but thought of a good cathedral city.

"Worms," she said.

Mr Lark started.

"Dead?" he asked hollowly.

"As far as I know, he's alive. You were saying, Mr Minkey — ?"

"This proposition," began Mr Minkey all over again, "isgoingtoappealtoanypersonofaverageintelligence."

He spoke so rapidly that the sentence sounded like a long and foreign word.

"Itmakesforeconomyofwork. Itreducestheoverhead – "

"Wait Minkey; I'll put it to the young lady so clearly that she'll see it before I'm through." Atterman smiled knowingly. "As a matter of fact, young lady, there's nothing to discuss. We've settled the terms, and this is just a formal meeting for fixing signatures."

"Hardly that, is it?" said Steele, the lawyer.

"Of course it isn't!" said Barbara scornfully. "Now listen to me, Mr Atterboy, and get this right: the only sale there's going to be in this house today is one which will be carried out in the proper place – over the counter. The deal is off."

Atterman swallowed something.

"Is that honourable?" he asked.

"It's both honourable and intelligent – " she began, but Julius leapt up in a fury.

"I'm not going to allow you to dictate to me," he said, shaking a fist at her. "What am I? Where do I come in?... Am I going to sit here and allow you to interfere with my business – with our business, I should say? I paid seven thousand pounds for a twenty-fifth share – seven thousand pounds." He thumped the table seven times. "If this deal doesn't go through, I am throwing up the business, and I want my money back. The whole thing is in decay. I haven't had a dividend since I've been in it. If you've got these almighty powers, dissolve my partnership, give me a cheque and let me out!"

To his amazement, the girl turned to the lawyer.

"Fix that, Mr Steele," said. "I'll give you a cheque tonight. I don't suppose he means it – "

"I mean every word of it," Julius was stung into saying. "Give me a formal declaration of dissolution and I'll sign it here and now!"

Barbara nodded to the lawyer, and with surprising rapidity he wrote out six lines, blotted it out carefully, and carried it to the end of the table.

"The cheque-book, Mr Lark."

Mr Lark uttered feeble sounds of protest.

'Cheque-book, Mr Lark!" she said, and he rose and crawled out, returning with a large flat book, which he placed before her.

Presently he would wake up and detect the cause of this terrible dream. He watched her, fascinated, saw her write "William Ebenezer Maber, by his attorney, Barbara Storr," beneath the polite instructions to the bank to pay Mr Julius Colesberg or at his order the sum of seven thousand pounds. The lawyer came to her for the cheque, examined it carefully, took it back to Julius, and he fixed his name to the document with a tremulous hand. Within an hour after signing his power of attorney, Mr Maber had lost a partner.

3

Barbara went out, ostensibly to lunch, in reality to perform a delicate duty.

In St James's Street was a block of small service flats, occupied in the main by wealthy bachelors. Mr Maber rented and occupied one of these. It was conveniently situated, and he had not the bother of maintaining a domestic staff. You pressed a bell once for the house waiter and ordered any food you required; pressed it twice for the house valet to brush your trousers. Mr Maber, who required a great deal of waiting upon, had bells within reach of his hand wherever he stood or sat.

She let herself in with the key he had given to her, and rang for the valet. She had been to the flat before to take Mr Maber's letters, and the man knew her.

"Mr Maber has been called away to the South of France," she said, "and he has asked me to send him on a change of clothes. Will you put one set of everything – one suit, one shirt…and all that sort of thing?"

"One set, miss?" said the miserable-looking valet. "What's the good of one set?"

"He can only wear one suit at a time," said Barbara with gentle patience.

"But he don't wear the same suit every day, miss – and he'll want a change of other things." The valet, a married man, approached the necessities with rare tact.

"He only wants one," said Barbara desperately. "He made a bet that he'll go round the world with only one suit."

The valet was intrigued; he was also suspicious.

"That's funny," he said. "I never knew that he was a betting man."

"Do you know anything, my good soul?" asked the exasperated Barbara. "Am I to cable to Germany and tell Mr Maber – "

"If he's going by way of Germany he'll never get round the world." The valet had a geographical mind. "I'll do it, miss," he said hastily as she made for the bedroom door.

She sat down and waited whilst he packed, and from time to time he thrust his head round the edge of the door and asked intimate questions.

"The summer weight," she said in answer to one query, and "Yes, braces," to another. You cannot spend your days in a store which has a men's department without penetrating mysteries which are hidden from the pure eyes of sheltered girlhood.

She carried the bag down the stairs after tipping Rupert magnificently, called a cab and drove to Marlborough Street police station.

"Yes, he's still here, and eating hearty," said the inspector, taking the bag from her. "We'll send the other things to you, unless you'd like to wait?"

"I'd rather not," said Barbara. "Will you send them to St. James's Street, inspector – no, to the office?"

Having supplied Mr Maber with the wherewithal in which he would rejoin his fellow-men in a month's time, she called at a restaurant, ate her frugal lunch and returned to the office.

Mr Julius Colesberg did not go out to lunch. He sat in his room, stunned, bewildered, before him a large cheque, in his mind the memory of that horrible five minutes when Barbara had risen with an "I think this concludes the business, gentlemen," and had swept out of the room. There was a piece of paper on the floor – Barbara possessed a tidy mind, and, stooping, had picked it up as she passed. He remembered this distinctly.

He recalled the sickly smile, scarcely human, upon the Lark's face; remembered the ominous words uttered by Mr Atterman as, with his lieutenant, he strode from the room.

There was a knock at the door and his typist came in.

"What do you want?" he growled.

"You told me to come for letters, sir," piped the girl.

"There are no letters," said Mr Colesberg dully. "There is no business. There is nothing. I am nothing – you are nothing. You are fired."

"What for?" demanded the indignant girl. "You can't fire me without giving me notice."

"Go and ask *her* to give you notice!" sneered Julius, and jerked his head towards the senior partner's room.

"Miss Storr?" A strange and unbelievable rumour had circulated through Maber & Maber. It was said that Mr Maber had secretly married Barbara Storr and had given the business to her as a wedding present. There were girls in the lingerie department who had seen the cake. The stoutish ladies in the mantle department met together behind screens of moire coats and wondered what the world was coming to. It was said that Mr Maber was so ashamed that he could never enter the office again. Others believed that they had parted at the church door and that this elderly Lothario, realising the rashness of his act, had fled to Germany, borrowing a pair of Atterman's horn-rimmed glasses to disguise himself.

Julius sat with his head between his hands, pondering, wondering, hypnotised. He had thrown away a good job. No dividend had been paid him, but the salary he received represented interest on an investment three times as large as he had made.

Alan Stewart came in a great hurry, flew up the stairs and without so much as "by your leave," dashed into the office where Barbara was sitting.

"You wonderful girl!" he said in amazement. "Is it true?"

"Have you got the space?" she asked.

"By the grace of heaven there's a full front page vacant in the *Daily Megaphone* – they were going to use it as a 'house ad.' Have you got the copy?"

The table was littered with it, and he picked up the scribbled sheets.

"A sale!" he said. "Why, Mabers have never had a sale!"

"They're going to have one now," she said briskly. "I've just called for the stock books, and we've got stuff here that goes well back to the reign of Alfred the Great. Will you put that in order for me?" she said hopefully. "I'm not quite sure of the spelling."

He made a few corrections.

"There are certainly two 'a's' in 'bargain,'" he said. "But my dear child" – he looked up, shaking his head – "you can't organise a sale in twenty-four hours."

"I'm no child – I'm a grown woman. Be respectful. And you know nothing whatever of my capabilities," said Barbara. "Before a week has passed there'll be nothing left in this store but public money."

He looked at the advertisement, looked at her, scratched his head, frowned, and exhibited other proofs of doubt and uncertainty.

"The sale time is over – I suppose you realise that? But – "

"Pass, friend, all's well," she said, and waved her hand to the door.

Alan Stewart was walking through the store before he realised that he had meant to ask her what had brought about this revolutionary change in the policy of Maber & Maber.

He had scarcely gone before Mr Lark came, hypnotised, numbed, somnambulistic.

"You're reinstated as buyer," said Barbara calmly. "I have nobody else. Get Atterman's catalogue, find out what is selling best, call up every wholesaler in London and buy the stocks they have on hand of the goods that Attermans sell. Mark everything at cost price – and hurry."

She called the managers of departments together and addressed a few pungent words to the assembly.

"Maber & Maber have come to life after a hundred years," she said. "The firm is now Maber, Maber *and* Maber! Engage any extra staff you require to deal with the rush which will begin tomorrow at eleven o'clock. Who is the alleged warehouse manager?"

"I am, miss," said a little man with a deep voice.

"I'm afraid I'm going to disturb your daily nap," she said. "Everything out of the warehouse has got to come into the shop. Mark all the lines for sale at five per cent above cost. The sale begins tomorrow."

Somebody made a timid reference to overtime.

"We shall work all night tonight; I'm having my bed brought here," said Barbara, and soon after dispatched a boy messenger for Myrtle.

She was immersed in the ancient stock-book when Julius strode in. He was pale but self-possessed. She looked up at the sound of the handle turning.

"I'll have a knocker put on that door," she said pointedly. "What are you doing in our up-to-date establishment?"

"I have decided not to resign," said Julius.

Barbara leaned back in her chair and laughed politely.

"I'm not going until I know what has happened to Mr Maber; and if you insist upon my leaving I shall go straight away to an editor I know and tell him the whole story."

"You might add this to your reminiscences," said Barbara.

She pulled open the drawer, took out a piece of paper and held it so that he could see it. There were three lines scrawled in pencil, undoubtedly written by Mr Colesberg – he recognised the note and remembered the circumstances of its writing.

> *Offer £110,000 at the most. The stock is worth £30,000.*
> *Don't offer a penny more.*

"How's that for conspiracy, Mr Julius Colesberg? How is that for *punica fides*? And in case your education has been neglected, I will tell you that means 'Punic faith,' an ironic term applied to the junior partners in the old-established firm of Caesar & Co."

"That was a purely personal note," protested Julius.

She put the paper back in the drawer and locked it ostentatiously.

"Send the reporter along to me," she said. "I'd like to run a good news story by the side of our ads."

"You're not advertising?" shrieked Julius.

"I refuse to discuss our business projects with a member of the opposition."

"Anyway, I'm not going." Julius was in rebellion. "I'm going to stay here until Maber comes back, and I defy you to move me! If you want a scandal you shall have one. Where is Maber?"

"In Cologne."

"You said Worms before. Now you've turned it into Cologne."

Barbara sighed wearily.

"Didn't you know that worms turn?"

"I'm going to find out – " began Julius.

There came a tap at the door, and the little office boy put his head in and made mysterious signals. Rising, puzzled, she went out, and confronted the tall, hollow-cheeked constable. He was carrying the bag she had left at the station.

"I've come, miss," he said simply. "The sergeant fixed it."

She gave a gasp of relief.

"Are you staying…on duty?"

He nodded.

"Leave the bag in the passage and come in here," she said, and went back to the office.

Julius started at the sight of the tall policeman; blinked from him to the girl.

"What – what – what – ?" he stammered. His voice had the sound of a water-bottle being emptied.

"Will you kindly put this man into the street, constable?"

Even the policeman was startled.

"This what?" he said.

"That what," said Barbara gravely.

The policeman opened the door and jerked his thumb to the corridor.

"Let him get his hat from the office; he may catch cold," said Barbara with womanly solicitude.

Julius staggered forth, a broken man…

The constable's name was A Sturman. She thought "A" stood for Arthur, or, at worst, for Augustus. He told her in all seriousness that it stood for "Albuera" – a name devoted to the young life by his father, an enthusiastic sometime sergeant of the Middlesex Regiment, to commemorate the great battle in which the 57th distinguished themselves. He added that very few people called him "Albuera," that his intimates referred to him as "Joe." He mentioned that he was single and was expecting promotion any day. He informed her that he knew many better things than patrol duty. That he lived with a married cousin in Notting Hill; that he had once spoken to the Prince of Wales; and that he came from a long-lived family. She could have written the story of his life after her first long interview with him.

The machinery of Maber & Maber was buzzing. She sensed the unaccustomed activity even from her eyrie. Mr Lark had left the office and was dashing madly in all directions. His typist, on the verge of tears, was inditing letters to the most unlikely people, asking them to supply at once, or to forward by passenger train, the fulfillment of all orders which had been suspended whilst the negotiations for the sale of the business were in progress. She was working by a list which Mr Lark had thrust at her before he dashed forth on his hectic mission. It was afterwards discovered that he had given her a list of people who owed money to the firm and were extremely unlikely to pay.

Slim goddesses no longer walked in stately idleness through the aisles of the ribbons, stockings and lingerie, admiring themselves in a sort of sad ecstasy before the long mirrors. They were dishevelled, hot, sucked pencils, made notes, even swooned.

The afternoon post came, and Barbara, sorting the letters, discovered amongst them one which had been delivered by hand and was marked "Very Urgent and Private." It was addressed to Mr Maber, and she hesitated before she opened it. It was a woman's hand. Barbara smiled softly. Poor Mr Maber! And yet, was he so poor? He was a happy man, with his hobbies, his church music and his memories of his beloved university.

Such men as he were born to be bachelors; to meander through life pleasantly; to enjoy the solitude of cosy rooms and an ordered existence; to find their quiet fun on the reaches and back-waters of smooth circumstance. They regretted nothing; saw the happiness of families, yet preferred their own joyous solitude.

She looked at the letter musingly. Some pensioner of his: he had scores of them – she herself had discovered a few. But there must be many unknown to her. He was very touchy about these letters marked "Personal" and "Private." The only time he had been really annoyed with her was when she had opened an envelope so inscribed, and had learnt that he was supporting the family of an old gardener.

The letter could not remain unanswered. She overcame the habit of long practice, put the stiletto through the flap and took out the letter. Instantly she was overwhelmed by the heady fragrance of "Sharimar,' that classy perfume which, to quote its advertisements, "brings to the dressing-table the roses of Kashmir – every bottle a garden."

She opened the letter wonderingly and at the first word nearly dropped it.

My own darling, beloved husband—

Barbara swayed; the room was behaving like an exhibition side-show. When she recovered she examined the envelope. Yes – *W E Maber, Esq. of Maber & Mabers*. There was no doubt whatever about that.

My own darling, beloved husband (she read slowly), *Why did you not call on me last Sunday? We had such a lovely joint for dinner! When can I see you, my precious? I count the hours when I am away from thee! And oh, my beloved darling, I'm getting so short of money. You know you promised faithfully to send me five hundred on Saturday. Is this the way to treat your wife? When I agreed to a secret marriage and promised that I would not speak to my dearest friend about it, I never dreamt that you would leave me so much alone. Do not run away from me. Ever thine, Margaret Maber.*

"Good God!" gasped Barbara, who was not as a rule given to profanity.

4

Mr Maber was married! He had been leading a double life! All Ilchester, all the world thought him a bachelor. Barbara ran her fingers through her hair; came perilously near to the vulgarity of scratching her head. She read the letter again. The handwriting was not Vere de Vere; the letter was badly expressed, jumped from expressions of undying love to the practical bread and butter of life.

The letter was on plain paper, the address being written at the top: "Hollyoak, Mantilla Road, Streatham." She remembered Mantilla Road; it was near the County Lunatic Asylum. How handy for Mr Maber!

She was puzzled how she knew the place at all, and then recalled the fact that there was a time when Mr Maber took a childish delight in watching the arrivals and departures of the Paris-London air service, that she had driven down with him across Tooting Common. Mantilla Road ended on the Common and the name was inscribed on a wall that could not be missed by the passer-by. She wondered what old Spanish don had christened this chaste thoroughfare, and after what dark-eyed beauty of Seville.

"I'm going mad," said Barbara, getting up and literally shaking herself.

But there was the grisly truth; she looked numbly at the letter. Mr Maber was married...had a wife...children perhaps? Otherwise, why the Sunday joint? Why not a steak or a chop?

There was a discreet knock at the door and Constable Albuera carried in the bag.

"Where will I put this, miss?"

She shook her head helplessly. Why not send it to Mantilla Road? With a note: "Dear madam, I enclose your husband's trousers, dress coat and shirt. Please acknowledge receipt."

"Put it – put it in the safe," she said.

"Through the keyhole?" asked Constable Albuera, who had once had a sense of humour.

She unlocked the big safe, threw the bag into its depths and slammed the door viciously.

"I put that fellow on the street," said the police officer. "I don't think he's right in the head. He kept saying, 'Where do I come in?' which was silly, considering he weren't coming in at all, but going out! Do you want anything, miss?"

"Go and bring the head of the silks department," she said.

"His head, miss?" asked the constable, aghast. "I'm not allowed by lore – "

"Ask Mr Gringer, head of the silks department, to come," said Barbara, blissfully unconscious of the stir that a constable in uniform would create in that serene atmosphere.

Albuera returned in a few minutes, bringing with him an ancient man, as pale as death, and whose teeth chattered audibly. Mr Gringer had been in the employ of the firm for forty-three years, and never before had he obeyed the crook of a stern policeman's finger. He staggered into Barbara's presence and almost collapsed upon the table.

"It's always been the practice of this house," he said in a high, quavering voice, "for the head of any department to be able to purchase goods from stock at cost price. The three blouses I took for my daughter-in-law last Saturday week are debited in my account, and I've got the book here – "

"That will do, Mr Sturman," and the constable retired discreetly, taking up a position outside the door in case he was required. "Sit down, Mr Gringer. You have known Mr Maber for many years, haven't you?"

"Yes, miss," said Mr Gringer, "and never once has he raised the slightest objection to my purchasing goods out of stock at cost price.

The white satin waist was slightly shop-soiled. I showed it to my chief assistant, and asked her if she thought it would be stretching a point if I marked it down to eight and three – "

"You were probably robbing yourself," said Barbara soothingly.

It took Mr Gringer some time to realise that no charge was pending and that he was not doomed, for the remainder of his declining years, to some damp and underground cell in Dartmoor Prison specially reserved for managers of departments who buy at cost price.

"Yes, Miss Storr," he said when he was calmer, "I've know Mr Maber for thirty-three years in July – either the second or the third, I'm not sure which."

"Never mind about the date. Have you ever been to his house in Ilchester?"

"Yes, miss. I once spent a delightful four days in that magnificent city."

"Obviously you didn't see much of it," said Barbara. And then: "How long has he been a bachelor?" she asked. "I mean, he's been a bachelor all of his life, hasn't he?"

"Yes, miss," said the amazed head of the silks, and added with native caution: "So far as I know. Mr Maber never confided his secrets to me. I shouldn't imagine that he'd been married before."

"Before what?" asked Barbara, startled.

Mr Gringer blushed and coughed.

"There is a story in circulation – and one sincerely hopes it is true – " he began, but Barbara fixed him with a steely eye, for a faint echo of that rumour had reached her. Tactfully she did not pursue a subject fraught with so much embarrassment for her companion.

Mr Gringer knew little or nothing of his employer's private life; that was plain. She turned the conversation to the forthcoming sale, and as soon as was convenient sent him back, a free man, to his pallid ladies, there to slay the authenticated rumour that he had been searched in Miss Storr's office and marked money had been found in almost every pocket.

Who would know? thought Barbara.

Julius? She was almost sorry she had had him thrown into the street. This thought of Julius must have had a telepathic origin, for the phone bell went as she meditated upon the possibility of getting information from that source. It was Mr Colesberg's voice, singularly mild, almost apologetic.

"I say, I'm afraid I've been an awful fool," he said. "Can't you forgive me and let us be friends? I'm sure you don't want to get the old man's back up?"

"Why do you call him 'old man'?" she asked suddenly, as a terrible thought flashed through her mind.

"Well, I regard him as a father," said Julius. "No disrespect was meant, I assure you."

And then an inspiration came to her.

"Is Colesberg your real name?" she asked quickly.

No answer came from the other end of the wire, and she repeated the question.

"Who's been talking about me?" demanded Mr Colesberg, obviously annoyed. "I do wish you wouldn't go prying into things which don't concern you."

The truth was that the name of "Colesberg" had been acquired by deed poll during the war. Previous to its adoption his patronymic had a distinct Teutonic flavour. Very few people and certainly not Mr Maber, knew that he had, by advertisement, announced to all and sundry that he would no longer be known as "Kolinzberger," but that was before he came to the firm of Mabers.

"It is my name now, anyway," he snapped.

Unless Barbara's ears deceived her, she had heard a murmur of expostulation and warning. Mr Colesberg became immediately conciliatory.

"You'll want a lot of help in this sale idea of yours," he said. "Why not let the question of partnership remain in abeyance, and allow me to come over and give you all the help I can?"

"What do you mean by 'come over'?" she asked. "Are you speaking from Attermans?"

"No," said Julius loudly.

She considered the matter and made her decision.

"You may return," she said, and hung up the phone.

So that was the ghastly truth. Colesberg was not his name. The presence of this exquisite in Mr Maber's office was now explained. Julius Colesberg was Mr Maber's son!

The discovery momentarily paralysed her activities. She sat with clasped hands, musing on the duplicity of the old man. Such cases had come within her knowledge; and always the villain of the piece had been a mild and likeable old gentleman whom one would never have suspected.

Barbara sighed deeply. She felt she had lost something in this new aspect of Mr Maber's character. And yet he could not be happily married. He had never spoken well of Julius, and when he had got into trouble he had not sent for his wife.

In the course of her meditations she heard one or two disturbances at the end of the passage, but took no notice, until Constable Albuera came in, slightly flushed.

"I've thrown him down the stairs three times, miss, but he says you want to see him."

"Who?" she gasped.

"That yellow-faced feller you told me to put out."

"Oh, good Lord!" Barbara remembered. "Let him come in, please."

Mr Julius Colesberg came in, dusty, dishevelled, his collar awry, his face hot and flushed.

"I want that man's number!" he demanded. "I'm going to write straight away to the Commissioner of Police, who is a personal friend of mine – "

"It was my fault; I forgot to take the bar off. Sit down, Mr Colesberg."

"You may go into your own room now," she said gently.

She thought that by virtue of her power of attorney she stood *in loco parentis*.

"You will resume with your salary, but the question of your partnership remains until Mr Maber returns from Rome."

"Has he gone to Rome now?" asked Julius, staggered.

"All roads lead to Rome," said Barbara indulgently.

At the time usually fixed for the closing of the store Mr Lark returned. The revolution in management had wrought a subtle change both in his character and demeanour. From being the calm manipulator of figures, and the languid buyer who interviewed travellers at his leisure, he had turned into a Force. Whether it was the influence of Mr Minkey, whom he secretly admired, or whether these dynamic qualities had lain dormant through the years and needed only the provocation of Barbara Storr to reach germination, it was certain that Mr Lark, who went out a little scared, very much bewildered and altogether incompetent, had returned, if not a captain of industry, at least a sergeant-major.

"I saw Green & Sterling," he said with unusual brightness. "I've taken their whole stock of petticoats, princess robes – " He enumerated the category, and Barbara, ordinarily a modest woman, listened unmoved. "I've seen Marks & Pearce and the Imperial Novelties, and cleared their stocks the very minute before Minkey arrived. I think I ought to tell you, Miss Storr, what the manager of the Imperial Novelties Company said to me. He said: 'Mr Lark, I've seen some live wires, but you're the livest.' " He beamed electrically.

"And I really believe you are," said Barbara slowly. "When will these goods be along – next Friday week?"

"They'll be here" – he tugged out his watch – "at seven. Special delivery – trollies – spare no expense. I'll have the warehouseman on the carpet if he has let a single man go after me telephoning him. And I've seen old Gordon Coke. He got a range of Paris models that were ordered by Atterman. Atterman tried to knock down the price after he'd got them because the linings were different to what he ordered, and sent them back. I've got 'em!"

He leaned negligently on the desk, his legs crossed, his eyes closed. Barbara looked round for a halo.

"You're wonderful!" she said in a hushed voice. "I really believe you're wonderful."

Mr Lark was thoughtful at this.

"I really believe I am," he admitted. "To tell you the truth, I never thought it was in me. I called at a printer's on the way and got some stock sale bills. I thought we'd plaster 'em up tonight. And what about a band?" he said daringly.

They looked at one another, the same thought, the same fear in their eyes.

"Isn't it rather – " she asked – "I mean…for Marlborough Avenue?"

"*He* has a band," said Mr Lark doggedly, "a syncopated orchestra – if you can call an orchestra a band."

"Maudie," she said.

He thought it was a polite cuss-word and smiled.

"I'll see to that, Mr Lark," said Barbara rapidly, reaching for the phone. "You've been a hero. Go down and hustle the managers. Take them out to dinner – I don't suppose they've ever had a square meal in their lives."

In Mr Lark's bosom had dawned a notable ambition.

"What about a manager?" he asked quietly and significantly. "There isn't one. I was a sort of licence officer – "

"Liaison?" she suggested, and he raised his eyebrows.

"Is that the word, Miss Storr? I thought it was something rude. Well, I'm that kind of officer between the shop and the office – what about me?"

"Appointed," said Barbara promptly. "Oh, by the way, I've let Mr Colesberg come back. He's in his room." And, as the new manager pursed his lips doubtfully: "There are – family reasons," said Barbara, averting her eyes.

Mr Lark nodded gravely.

"I understand," he said, understanding nothing.

Mr Atterman's private office was situated on the fifth floor of his palatial building, and commanded not only a view of the street but of the room where, concealed behind green silk half-curtains, Barbara had established herself. Mr Atterman and his Live Wire stood in thoughtful silence, looking down upon the decorous facia of Maber & Maber.

"It's a flash in the pan – a mere flash in the pan," said Mr Atterman at last. "She'll get it all tangled up, and by the time the old man comes back there won't be any business."

Yet he was uneasy: the news which his lieutenant had brought was the reverse of comforting.

"If you had the brains of a jack rabbit you'd have stepped right in and bought before that woolly-headed clown had signed an order. Now listen, Minkey! This thing has got to stop right now. I don't care what it costs, clear all the floating stock from every wholesaler – make it so that she can't get so much as a shirt-waist inside a month. And have those dresses we sent back to Gordon Coke."

"I can't," breathed Mr Minkey; "she's got 'em!"

The head of the house of Atterman described Mr Minkey in language which was unfamiliar to the Live Wire.

"Now go out and rustle up these dry goods people. If their stores are closed, find out where they live and see them. You needn't take any stuff off their hands – stall 'em. Get an option. Only keep the stuff from going into Mabers."

"What is Colesberg doing?" asked Mr Minkey resentfully.

"That's none of your business," snapped Atterman. "I'm feeling happier in my mind now that he's on the job."

An assistant came hurriedly to him, said something in a low voice, and Mr Atterman followed the messenger swiftly to his beautiful office, where all that was not gilt was crimson plush. Over the beautiful marble mantelpiece was a great photograph of the Statue of Liberty, before which Mr Atterman might often have been discovered standing, a beatific expression on his face. It was the one part of America he had seen distinctly. Near by, and out of range of the camera, was a little spot on earth called Ellis Island, which he knew much better, having spent three disagreeable weeks thereon prior to his deportation. But this was before he had started business in the little shop in Islington and had laid the foundation of the fortune which had brought him to the aristocratic neighbourhood of Marlborough Avenue.

His visitor was a middle-aged man from a well-known private inquiry office. Mr Atterman pushed a box of cigars towards him and sat down.

"You've got agents in Germany?"

The visitor nodded.

"I'll tell you what I want you to do." Mr Atterman bent forward over his desk. "I want to find Mr Maber. He's gone abroad somewhere, and I believe he's gone to Germany – Worms or Cologne. Get the wire busy. And you go down to his house in Ilchester and make a few enquiries. The old fox may have crept back to the country after giving his secretary full power to act for him. He's got a flat in St. James's Street, too: put in an inquiry there."

"And when we've found him?" said the agent.

"Let me know his address, and I'll go after him."

The agent rose.

"Who is this girl – what has she to do with it?" he asked.

Briefly, Mr Atterman explained the situation.

"She may know; on the other hand, she may not," he said. "You've – got – to – find – Maber!"

This business settled to his satisfaction, he took up the telephone, gave Mabers' number, and asked the private exchange to switch him through to Julius.

"So you're settled?"

"I'm settled all right," grumbled Julius. "I simply hate the idea of being in that loathsome place with this perfectly awful girl."

"What are you doing?" asked Atterman.

"Nothing," snarled Julius. "Just sitting there like a fool."

"Hang on – that's all, hang on!"

Having issued his commands, Mr Atterman hung up the telephone, and for the next half-hour lounged about his mammoth store. And, as a needle to a magnet, so was he drawn to that corner of the roof restaurant which such a popular feature of his establishment, where the Luisiana Ladies' Orchestra, in scarlet coats and hats, were making music for the multitude. He leaned against a pillar and watched the cornet soloist who had taken the place of one who had a very real hold on him, despite the expense to which she had put him (the judge disallowed his costs), despite the contempt, hatred and malice of a momma who had a young lady named Rachel Sibinski in her eye, and the guttural malignity of a stepmother who would never be happy until she had seen him with Nitiska Something-ending-in-Koski in the synagogue.

Mr Atterman had that streak of sentimentality which is the proper possession of all great minds. He thought of Maudie, with her golden hair and her china-blue eyes, and that little dimple that used to come into her cheeks as she rendered her *obbligatos*. He had forgiven the base treachery of the girl, who had endeavoured to rob him of something which was dearer than life – her claim was for five thousand pounds – and thought only of those innocent rides of theirs, her trusting hand in his, her lips, designed by nature and educated by years of practice on the cornet, against his cheek. He sighed again. She loved him…that was the thought which made his heart grow tender towards her, even in his bitterest moments.

One momma pointed out to him how great merchant princes could only marry great ladies; they instanced the case of the monumental mason of Oxford Street, who had married into the aristocracy, his wife's father being a Sir. They pointed out the lowness and debasing influences of the cornet, and they openly sneered at him when he talked of her art.

If, instead of standing by the orchestra, he had walked to one of the many front doors of the building, he would have seen the object of his thoughts descent from a No. 9 bus and pass into the rival establishment. Maudie Deane tripped upstairs, cast an anxious and apprehensive eye at the policeman, and was warmly greeted by the new head of Mabers.

"Maudie, what was Atterman's favourite tune?"

"His favourite tune, my dear?" Maudie was rather taken back. "He liked 'Let me like a soldier fall,' but I think his favourite tune was 'Less than the dust beneath thy chariot wheels.' "

Barbara strolled up and down the apartment, the awe and wonder of Myrtle, summoned from her peaceful occupation of cleaning the knives and sitting now gingerly on the edge of a chair.

"Which is his office – Atterman's?"

Maudie walked to the window and pointed up. There was a light burning in the room, but at that moment Mr Atterman was sentimentalising near the orchestra.

"I think that will do," said Barbara slowly. "I want you to come tomorrow prepared to sit on the roof and play his favourite airs."

"Good heavens! Why?" asked Maudie.

"I may not want you to do it; it all depends," said Barbara. "The thing is, I may wish to discover whether the man has a human soul; whether he has any sense of gratitude for past favours; whether the divine – anyway, will you do it, Maudie?" she asked practically.

Maudie's eyes were alight. Secretly she hugged the belief that there abode in the grooves and hollows of the fearsome brass a siren voice which would enchant the man. She had seriously considered the possibility of playing outside the shop, and had even made enquiries as to whether this was an offence under the Street Noises Act.

"What time shall I come?"

"At nine," said Barbara. "It is a flat roof, and if it's raining I'll have a tent put up."

She jotted down "tent" on her blotting-pad.

She had not carried out her threat to bring her bed, but she was on the premises until nearly midnight, watching a galvanised staff dressing windows behind the drawn shades, consulting the new manager, who proved surprisingly intelligent and earned more respect in that night than he had lost in the four years she had known him.

Julius, weary-eyed and bored, came to watch the amazing scene, until he could stand it no longer, and drifted out to his club. Even Albuera lent a hand, his official duties being at an end for the day. In his shirt-sleeves he was less impressive, but infinitely more helpful. Myrtle was frankly useless. She could neither handle nor pack. She retired early to help in the kitchen.

Near on midnight, Mr Stewart came with the damp proof of the front page.

"You know, of course, that will cost…?"

He mentioned a sum that made Barbara go pale; she began to understand Mr Maber's antipathy to advertising.

"But it will bring you probably ten times as much." He added this comforting assurance when he saw her stagger. "Mabers have never had a sale. You were wise to emphasise that. I can give you another page tomorrow and a half-page on Wednesday. You have the luck of the beginner: not once in a thousand years could you find two and a half pages empty a day or so before you wanted them. How long is the sale to last, by the way?"

"Till we've sold all the old stock and most of the new," she said promptly. "The Lark is wonderful!"

"Is that him singing now?" asked Alan.

Mr Lark was addressing the warehousemen in terms of violent reproach.

"That is him," said Barbara, with a happy sigh. "I wish I could say those things!"

"Where *is* Mr Maber?"

It was the first opportunity he had for pressing home the question.

"He has gone to America," she said absently. "I wonder whether I ought to take those pages. Yes, I will! I've got eight hundred wonderful models – Mr Lark only bought them late today, and I simply *must* talk about them!"

"But does he *know* you're doing these alarming things?" he asked. "I feel horribly guilty; I put this advertising bug into your brain, and yet – "

"And yet I may be doing right?" she smiled tiredly. "You can wait now and take me home; Myrtle is here and will chaperon me. She thinks I'm drinking."

It was half-past twelve when, with scarcely the energy to climb the stairs, she reached her flat and undressed in her sleep.

"Your tea, miss…"

The bright sunlight flooded the little room. Barbara sat up suddenly and said:

"We ought to have a window display – something snappy."

She stared at Myrtle as at a stranger and laughed.

I've had the weirdest dream, Myrtle. I dreamt that Mr Maber had been locked – "

Her eyes fell upon a great pile of delivery notes stacked upon the table. She had brought them home with her, intending to check them before she went to bed. It was true, then! No phantasmagoria of a diseased or weary brain. He *was* locked up! In Pentonville.

She looked at the clock; it was exactly seven. Mr Maber would be picking oakum now. How sweet! Her pyjamaed legs swung out of bed and she drank the hot tea at a gulp.

"I've got the paper, miss."

Barbara snatched it from her and gazed in rapture on the first of her literary compositions to gain the honour of print. How perfectly splendid! She wrote that big page. A million, even two million, people would be reading it at that moment – or a little later. Reading what she had written! She read every announcement with the pride of authorship.

Crêpe Georgette! In saxe, salmon, gold, electric, pink and nigger. 3/11.

and

Ladies' Smart Velour Coats. Just the thing for the chilly nights. Tailored on quiet, plain lines, with button and loop collar of beaver coney. 21/-.

and also:

Evening Wrap in rich blue chiffon velvet, lined throughout with rich silk in effective moonlight shades. Full-necked collar; a few only. 37/6.

"How perfectly marvellous!" crooned Barbara, raising her eyes in ecstasy to the ceiling. "And Attermans are offering them at five guineas!"

She leapt up, set the bath-tap running, and returned to the examination of her newspaper... Myrtle was providentially passing the bathroom in time to pull the waste button just as the water was welling over the edge.

A hasty breakfast, while Myrtle sought and found a taxi, and then a quick flight to the store.

And now the reaction had come. Would anybody read the advertisement, and, reading, would they take the slightest notice of it? The question was answered when she came in sight of the store. Two policemen were marshalling a long queue of women who had apparently stayed up all night in order to get the first news of any sale which was sprung on them.

It was eight o'clock: Mabers opened at nine. Yet, early as was the hour, Mr Lark was on duty, shaved, spruce, and, if a little haggard, enthusiastic.

"I took rooms for the girls at the hotel on the corner" he said. "Couldn't afford to risk their being late. My young lady has gone round to call 'em. Atterman's been here."

He enjoyed the sensation he created.

"Yes, half an hour ago. Came to the staff door and asked for me. Offered me twenty a week and a year's contract to go over the road."

"What did you say?" asked Barbara in a hushed voice.

"I told him to go to aitch," said Mr Lark politely.

"Where's that — oh, you mean hell? Shake!"

They shook hands solemnly.

"Your salary is up to twenty and you're allowed to wear a top hat in business hours," she said.

The first thing she saw when she pulled open the drawer of her desk gave her a little shock. It was Mrs Maber's letter. Something must be done about that. Steele! Of course, she ought to see Mr Maber's lawyer at once. She jotted down "Steele" under "tent" and wondered why she had written "tent."

Julius, arriving at nine-fifteen, had to fight his way through a solid mass of fierce women, and, once in the shop, had to elbow diligently to reach the office stairs.

On the top landing stood Barbara, the light of triumph in her eye. Behind her, looming out of the gloom, the cadaverous countenance of PC Albuera Sturman.

"I've had to send for more police." Barbara was outwardly calm. "All the novelty marocain went by half-past eight, and there isn't a pair of stockinette – some of the stock has gone. They haven't seen the Paris models yet."

Julius puffed gloomily.

"This sort of thing can't go on," he said. "It isn't worth the bother – we're selling at a loss; the end of that is ruin." He shook his head.

"You're a little ray of sunshine, aren't you?" Barbara scoffed. "The stock is worth thirty thousand. You said so. Mr Maber was prepared to take twelve. If I sell it for more than thirty – "

Again he shook his head.

"You won't. This sort of thing looks all right on paper – but don't you think, if there was anything in it, the old man would have done this years ago? Take my advice: before you go any farther call in Atterman and consult him. You've ruined the reputation of the business – lowered it. You've brought it down, so to speak, from the Bond Street level to the level of High Street, Pimlico. You've damned Mabers for everlasting – "

"There's no call to use that language," said Albuera with official severity, and Barbara nodded her agreement.

"Go to your room, Julius," she said in her motherly way, "and if you're good I'll let you count the money."

So far from dwindling, the crowd gathered in volume. There were now policemen at the doors to regulate the influx according to the capacity of the premises. Every cash desk was transferring incredible sums to Mr Lark's office, and his stenographer sat behind ragged ramparts of crumpled bills, weeping silently at the knowledge of her own inadequacy.

As for Mr Lark, he had recommenced his daily task. Twice he met the Live Wire coming into a wholesaler's as he was coming out. Minkey grinned fiendishly at him on each occasion. It was a great day for the Lark. He was the livest wire; in comparison Mr Minkey was a mere telephone connection, *sans* volts, *sans* amperes, *sans* watts, *sans* everything.

There had never been such a sensational happening in the history of the soft-goods trade. The proprietors of other stores either came personally or sent their trusted representatives to examine the phenomenon at first hand. Some of them consulted respectfully with Mr Atterman, and even accepted the hospitality of his ornate office, where the operations of this ancient intruder into the modern system of salesmanship could be observed.

"It is a flash in the pan," said Mr Atterman moodily. "Half these people are shoplifters, and the other half are drawn by curiosity."

"I should never have thought that Maber would have taken this course," said a magnate from Regent Street.

"It is not him," replied Mr Atterman, with a fine disregard for the rules of grammar; "it's that upstart girl of his. There's something behind this," he added darkly.

From time to time he received confidential messages from his agent. Julius was frankly flabbergasted, not so much by the volume of business as by Barbara's attitude.

"I can't understand her letting me come back," he said, "unless she's scared of what the old man will say when he turns up. She comes in every half-hour to tell me the takings. I've never known her so civil before."

"She wants to get the right side of you," said Atterman. "Now listen, Colesberg: you've got to put your foot down. What did you say the figures were?"

Julius told him, and Mr Atterman whistled.

"As much as that? I'll tell you what you're to do: write to all the wholesalers, and send your letters by special messenger, signing 'em 'junior partner,' and saying that you will not be responsible for any goods delivered to the order of Miss Barbara Storr. Send some of your note-heading over here. I'll have the letters written, you can sign them, and we'll have a corps of messengers to rush them all over London. Draw up the draft and send it with the notepaper; I'll do the rest."

"What good will that do?" asked Julius.

Mr Atterman did not say what he thought.

"Don't you see, you poor...foolish man, that if we can stop supplies – and these wholesalers are as scared as cats – Mabers won't even be able to replace the stocks for normal trading? Maber is not at Ilchester, and he's not at his flat. I've got men combing Germany for him. Now get busy."

Before Julius could get busy he must locate the girl. He had no desire to be interrupted in the act of repudiating her orders – she had eyes as sharp as a cat's. He strolled nonchalantly into her room and found her immersed in the preparation of tomorrow's advertisements.

"Just wait," she said, without looking up.

Julius just waited, and, waiting, he glanced across to the safe. The door was ajar, and he saw something and started. It was a big brown bag – Maber's travelling bag. He had seen it a dozen times before. What was that doing in the safe?

Barbara looked up suddenly, saw the direction of his eyes, guessed what he had seen and, rising swiftly, closed the safe door and turned the key.

"Now, Mr Colesberg?" she said in that conciliatory tone which had become habitual.

"I only want to say this," said Julius, clearing his throat, "that what you're ordering now you're ordering on your own responsibility. I absolutely refuse either to sanction or to endorse your orders."

"My dear Mr Colesberg," she said gently, "you have no *locus standi*. Your endorsement and approval aren't even asked. Of course you're not responsible."

"I only want to say – "

"Wouldn't you rather write me a note?" she said. "I'm very busy."

He stalked out, having obtained self-absolution in advance for the deed he contemplated.

Nobody knew better than Julius that such letters, signed by himself and broadcast through London, would paralyse supplies. His name was known in connection with the business; he was familiar to most of the leading houses. Julius pulled a virgin sheet of paper towards him and began writing.

For the moment the literary activities of his "senior partner" were suspended. Julius had seen the bag. Would he suspect anything? She cogitated. Before she could reach a definite conclusion, Albuera put his head in the door. He had given up knocking.

"A lady to see you, miss."

"A lady?" Barbara frowned. "Who?"

"She said she wants to see you very particular." He winked. "I think you'd better see her," he said ominously, and pushed the door open.

There came into the room a lady of thirty, very highly coloured, brass-headed, pink-cheeked, buxom. She was dressed in the height of the fashion which prevailed at the moment in the Brixton Road. Across her bosom was a large and flashing brooch, simply and tastefully made up of the words "Baby Mine." They might have been diamonds; they were certainly conspicuous.

"Miss Storr, I understand?" She raised her eyebrows inquiringly.

"That is my name," said Barbara. "Do you wish to see me?"

The lady closed the door carefully, pulled up a chair and sat down.

"May I harsk," she said with dignity, "what is your business sitting in my 'usband's armchair and a-reading of his letters?"

Barbara gasped.

"You're Mrs Maber?" she asked hollowly.

"That is my name – my card." She opened a large patent leather envelope bag ("eight and eleven, Bon Marché," said Barbara mentally), took out a card and passed it across the table. Barbara read:

Mrs Maber, 304, Mantilla Road, Tooting.

"I've come," said Mrs Maber, still employing the somewhat stilted and dignified attitude she had maintained from the first, still speaking deliberately, if a little inaccurately, "I've come to harsk and demand what you have done with my 'usband's money that he left for me."

"I think I can explain – " began Barbara.

Mrs Maber raised her head.

"Explanations I will not 'ave," she said inconsistently. "What have you done with my 'usband's money?"

Barbara did not hesitate; she pressed the bell, and, to the office boy who came:

"Ask Mr Colesberg to come in."

Apparently the word "Colesberg" meant nothing to the stout lady, for she did not flinch. In a few seconds Julius came though the door.

"Do you want me?" he asked.

Barbara pointed to the lady.

"Your mother," she said simply.

Julius glared at the visitor.

"My what?" he squeaked.

"Explain to her the position."

Mrs Maber had risen, red of face.

"What's the idea?" She was no longer languid or genteel. Her voice was harsh and threatening. "I got no children. What do you mean?"

Barbara looked from one to the other.

"Isn't this your son?" she asked. "Isn't he Mr Maber's son?"

"No!" said Mrs Maber and Julius in unison.

"You're not Mr Maber's son?"

"Mr Maber's son!" Julius was demoniacal in his wrath. "What the devil do you mean?"

"Are you or aren't you?" asked the exasperated girl.

"No!" yelled Julius.

"That simplifies matters – you've lost your *raison d'être*," said Barbara, and beckoned the waiting Constable Albuera, pointing to Julius. "Throw him into the street!" she hissed.

5

The sound of scufflings and expostulations grew fainter. Presently Police-Constable Albuera returned, a calm, phlegmatic man, with the quiet smile of one who had achieved that which he set out to achieve.

"All right, miss," he said, and touched his helmet.

"Thank you, Albuera," said Barbara gravely. She felt that in the circumstances it would have been an act of stiff formality to have called him anything but by his Christian name.

Mrs Maber was an interested and somewhat agitated spectator, and the presence of this representative contributed considerably to her uneasiness. She got up and closed the door again.

"Now, my dear," she said, and her tone was altogether different, "I don't want any unpleasantness, and I'm sure you don't. My husband, William Maber, told me that he was sending me five hundred pounds to purchase the new Rolls Royce motor car which I've been simply pining for munce an' munce."

"I always thought they were a little more expensive than that," said Barbara suspiciously.

"I'm getting it on the 'ire-purchase system," explained Mrs Maber glibly. "My dear, don't let us have any bother or argument. I know very well that my 'usband will be simply wild with me when he finds I've come up. But what am I to do? There's Mr Rolls standing on the doorstep waiting – "

Barbara looked at the hectic lady thoughtfully.

"Don't you think you'd better see Mr Steele?" she asked. "Who's Steele?" demanded the woman sharply.

"He's Mr Maber's solicitor. Surely you know that?"

Mrs Maber was silent.

"I know the man you mean," she said. "Mr Steele doesn't know me. The marriage was secret owin' to a death in the family; I was married in half-mournin'." And then, with a sudden burst of confidence: "I'm going to tell you the truth, my dear. Willie and I – "

"Who's Willie? Oh, Mr Maber – yes?"

"Well, Willie and I are not very 'appy, and when I asked him for the money for the motor car it was, so to speak, a mere – what's the word?"

"Subterfuge?" suggested Barbara.

"That's the word. I want to go abroad and travel. To tell you the truth, I don't want to see Willie any more. There, that's out, and I'm glad I've told you."

She sat back with an air of relief. Barbara was in a dilemma. It was dreadful to think that Mr Maber had married this vulgar creature, but the case was not exactly without parallel. There was Sir Olby Wustart, who had married his cook, and an eminent lawyer who had made even a worse *mésalliance*. And men of Mr Maber's age did these queer things; they went a little mad at a certain stage of life, or else the commonness in them could no longer be bottled up and must find expression in such choices.

Mrs Maber was fanning herself with her bag, her dark twinkling eyes fixed upon Barbara.

"Of course, I'm not going to say anything about the double life that Willie's been leading," she said. "I'm broad-minded. I'm not going to say anything about your being in charge of this business – "

"I hope you're not," said Barbara. "I should hate to have to call upon my police reserves. Now, Mrs Maber, the best I can do for you is to give you a hundred pounds, and that must be sufficient for you until I can get in touch with Mr Maber."

"A hundred isn't much," said the lady, and yet her sprightliness and the twinkle in her eye belied her hasty disparagement. "It will be all right on account, but, my dear, I simply must have more – "

"What is your Christian name, Mrs Maber?"

"Couldn't I have cash?" urged the lady, frowning at the cheque-book.

"I will make the cheque open. Your name is Margaret, isn't it?"

She wrote: "Pay to the order of Margaret Maber the sum of one hundred pounds," signed it, tore out the cheque and passed it across the table.

"I suppose you couldn't get somebody to cash this for me? I mean, I don't want the scandal of my name being on a cheque."

"Nobody will know – you may be his sister, or his – his daughter," she said flatteringly.

Still Mrs Maber wasn't pleased. She took up the cheque and examined it with an expression of doubt.

"All right," she said, "if that's the best you can do."

She went out, leaving the room slightly perfumed. Barbara opened the windows; she hated Sharimar ("every bottle a rose garden.").

So that was that. She was relieved of her responsibility for Julius. She went into his room to make sure that he hadn't sneaked back. He was gone. On his table was the rough draft of the letter which he had been writing when he had been interrupted, and she did not disdain to read this composition. No sooner had she read it than she was tearing back to her room. By great good fortune, Mr Lark chose that moment to return.

"Send a wire to every wholesaler in London," she said breathlessly, "and don't lose a minute."

She wrote the message quickly:

Mr Julius Colesberg is no longer connected with the firm of Maber & Maber, the partnership having been dissolved.

She rang up Steele, the lawyer, and was too intent upon the new development to tell him about Mrs Maber. That required a calmer and a saner attitude of mind that she could command.

"Send a letter to Julius Colesberg – you'll probably find him at Atterman's – telling him that if he represents himself as being associated with Maber & Maber you will apply immediately for a – what's the word?"

"An injunction?" suggested Steele, and then: "What's wrong?"

She told him briefly.

"You weren't wise in letting him come back," was all the comfort she received. "All right, Miss Storr, I'll send the letter by special messenger. What about Maber – any news of him?"

"None," she said. "He's still in – wherever he is."

This business finished, she fell back in her chair, exhausted. Running a business was not the fun she had anticipated.

"Fortunately," Julius was saying to the scowling Atterman, "I've plenty of the firm's note-paper at my house, and I've sent home for it. As for her policeman, I'm going to have the coat from his back, by heaven! Look at my collar!"

"I've seen it," said Atterman laconically, and then: "Maber isn't in Worms and he isn't in Cologne – and, what is more" – he tapped Julius impressively – "he's not abroad!"

"What!" said Julius in surprise.

"He's not abroad," said Atterman. "That inquiry agent of mine got hold of the valet at St James's Chambers, took him out and they had a drink together. Maber's passport is still at the flat, and without a passport and *visa* he couldn't possibly get into Germany and couldn't leave England."

Julius Colesberg stared incredulously at his informant.

"Then where is he?" he asked.

"Ah!" said Mr Atterman mysteriously. "That is what I'm going to find out! We've got a lot of information from the valet." He took no little credit to himself for this piece of detective work. "Yesterday afternoon Storr came to the flat and ordered this man to pack a bag with one complete change for the old man – just one change, mark you!"

"And did he pack it?"

Mr Atterman nodded.

"It was packed and taken away by Storr."

Suddenly Julius smacked his fist into his palm.

"I've got it! The bag is in the safe."

"She didn't send it on to him?" said Atterman in surprise. "That upsets my theory."

"The bag is in the safe, and, what is more, there's something wrong," cried Julius. "The moment she saw I'd spotted the grip, she jumped up and slammed the door. I never say anybody so confused and nervous as she was."

They looked at one another across the table.

"That's queer," said Atterman slowly. "My own idea was – well, it doesn't matter about that. In the safe? Why is it there? What is she keeping it for?"

Julius bit his nails savagely.

"What a fool I am!" he said. "I've a duplicate key of the safe. I could have waited until she was out and had a look at it – I'll bet we should find something else there which would give us a clue."

It was true that Julius had a duplicate key to the safe. Except for the day's takings, which were placed there at night, there was nothing in the safe but books and documents of no special value, and sometimes, especially Saturdays, when Mr Maber did not turn up at the office, it was necessary that the takings should be put in a secure place. He fished the key from his pocket now – a flat key attached to the end of his watchguard – and Mr Atterman eyed it thoughtfully.

"Have you a pass-key?" he asked.

Julius nodded.

"You mean to the store? Yes, I have a pass-key."

"Is there a night watchman?"

Mr Colesberg began dimly to understand.

"Ye-es," he said, "there's a night watchman, but he knows me very well, and unless Miss Storr calls the staff together and tells them I'm not to be admitted – even then I think he would make no fuss."

"Go tonight. Take Minkey with you," said Mr Atterman. "You'll want somebody to keep a look-out. In any case, you can always find an excuse for being there – say that you had left something behind. And anyway, there'll be no kick."

Julius did not accept the suggestion with alacrity.

"Isn't there another way of doing it – " he began.

Mr Atterman would hear of no other way; he dismissed the matter as definitely and finally settled.

Soon after this his courier came back from the house with a thick wad of Maber & Maber note-heading, and for the next hour Julius was busy dictating and signing letters addressed to the leading wholesalers of the metropolis, whilst a small army of messenger boys draped themselves along the wall of the corridor. The last letter had been signed when an earnest young man drifted into the room. He was the youth whom Barbara had seen at the police court on the morning of Mr Maber's fall.

"Mr Colesberg?" he asked, and Julius recognised him as a clerk from Steele, the solicitor, and his heart sank.

Tearing open the letter which was handed to him, he read it through, and Atterman saw by his face that something serious had happened.

"That will do," he said savagely, and the clerk withdrew. "What do you think of this?" He passed the letter across the table.

We are instructed by our clients, Messrs Maber & Maber, to inform you that, your partnership in that firm having been voluntarily dissolved and your association with that business having automatically terminated, you are no longer in authority to act for and on behalf of that firm; and we are instructed to take immediate steps to prevent your ordering or countermanding orders on behalf of and as a partner to Messrs Maber & Maber, or describing yourself as a director, manager, or partner in that business.

Yours faithfully,
Steele & Steele

"That's pretty plain," said Atterman. "I guess we can't get past that without raising a whole lot of trouble for ourselves. I wonder if she's got in ahead?"

He took up the telephone and gave a number, and when it was through handed the instrument to Julius.

"Tell them who you are, and that you want to countermand an order for a line of goods," he whispered.

Julius obeyed.

"I'm sorry, Mr Colesberg, but I've had a wire from your firm saying that you're no longer connected with the business and that we're to take no orders from you," was the reply. "We tried to call you up to ask you if this was so. Is it a fact?"

For a second Julius was tempted to issue an official denial, but his heart failed him.

"Quite true," he mumbled, and hung up the receiver.

"We'll wait till tonight," said Mr Atterman hopefully, but Julius felt less inclined for the adventure than ever.

When Mrs Maber left the premises occupied by her husband's business she called a cab and ordered him to drive to Marble Arch. She did not alight when she reached that venue, but beckoning a shabby little man who had been perambulating up and down the sidewalk for the past half-hour, an object of suspicion to the point constable, she opened the door and he jumped in.

"Well, did you get it?" he asked eagerly.

"I got a hundred," said the woman, and the face of Mr Hammett, the solicitor, fell. "A hundred's a hundred – I didn't expect to get that."

"Did you tell her about the motor car?" asked Mr Hammett as she fumbled in her bag for the cheque.

"I told her about the motor car and wanting to go abroad," said the woman. "I think I was a fool not to tell the truth at first. Have you got the tickets?"

He nodded gloomily.

"A hundred's no more use to me than a kick in the neck," said Mr Hammett without elegance. "I've got twenty-five judgments out against me, and this time I'm going off the rolls – sure! If you'd only stuck out you'd have got the five hundred."

"I was scared to death," confessed the woman. "That girl's got an eye like a hawk. And why you should think she was pretty, God knows!"

"What's this?" asked Hammett with a frown as she handed him the slip of paper.

"It's a cheque, made payable to bearer."

"Made payable to you – to Margaret Maber, you fool!" he said roughly. "You can't cash this."

"Why not?" she gasped.

"Because if you do they'll pinch you for forgery – that's why!" stormed the man. "You great simpleton, why didn't you get money – real money?"

The lady who for fifteen years, and ever since she had graced the saloon bar of the "Crown and Anchor" in the Waterloo Road, had been Mrs Hammett (and she had her marriage lines to prove it) began to weep softly.

"It is the best idea that I've ever struck. You could have got five hundred – you could have got a thousand out of her if you'd had the brains of a gnat!" raved the little man. "I'll have the railway tickets dated for tomorrow. You go up and see her and we'll cash both cheques together. We might as well be hung for a sheep as a lamb. And anyway, the old boy wouldn't prosecute," he added, brightening up. "He's doing a month in 'stir,' and he won't want to advertise that fact."

"Why not cash this today?" she asked, shaking the slip.

"No, we won't make two bites at one cherry. Both cheques have got to come out together. I'll fix a yarn for you that ought to draw a thousand – what's more, it will be true."

And Mr Hammett, who had mixed law and blackmail all his life, and diluted both practices with neat whisky, unfolded his plan.

This was a memorable day in the life of Barbara Storr. From time to time she pushed up the window of her office and leaned out to observe the crowd. All Bayswater was there, and Pimlico and West Kensington, to say nothing of Balham, Lewisham and Kilburn. The Londoner has a keen scent for a bargain, and when Barbara had decided to sell at five per cent above cost, and in some cases at two per cent above cost, she had introduced cuts and changes of a most startling and attractive character. That blessed man, Alan Stewart, had begged or borrowed eighty "bus sides." The failure of two plays simultaneously had left space for the brief announcement, "Staggering Reductions at Mabers' Sale." The omnibuses bearing this bill began to be observable that afternoon. The sandwich-board men had been perambulating the busy streets since early morning. Alan called and was consulted as to the window display. Barbara had cleared one window, and in this she intended to put something which would gather the crowds more densely and could not fail to produce the inevitable summons for obstruction.

"It ought to be something alive and moving," said Barbara. "What about a lion?"

"A what?" said Alan, aghast.

"You can hire tame lions. Maudie Deane got acquainted with a lion-tamer at one of her vaudeville shows. She says you can get lions that will eat out of your hand."

He shook his head.

"I don't think so. You might frighten the people. And besides, it would take you weeks to get a proper cage fitted."

He went away to investigate, and eventually got into touch with a showman's agent.

"I've the very thing – a Wild Man from Borneo! In fact I've got a couple on my books," said the agent.

"That's an ancient idea."

"People like ancient ideas," said the agent truly. "And besides, these fellows haven't had an engagement in London for years, and it might be a bit of novelty."

By the time Alan reached the agent's office the two wild men had dwindled to one, the less desirable man having found an engagement that morning. There was half an hour's wait before the showman's emissary had rounded up Okko. He had been discovered in a bar and was slightly intoxicated, Alan thought. Below middle height, a wild tangle of hair and a beard that seemed to sprout in all directions made him a fearsome and terrifying object. Low-browed, with eyes that twinkled savagely, he waved his long and hairy arms in protest when the project was put before him.

"I'll do anything in town, but I won't do a shop-window act," he said in a shrill Cockney voice. "When you said 'London' I thought you meant the halls. The idea of me lowering my dignity by sitting in a shop window...it can't be done!"

"Now listen, Okko," said Mr Lazarus soothingly. "This is certain to get you a big engagement. We've turned down every other wild man, and there are dozens – "

"There are only two," said Okko sulkily, "and Bill Miles has got an engagement with the Wild Prairies Circus outfit – they're starring him as a prehistoric man. Don't try any of that stuff with me. It's lowering the profession, and I'm not going to do it."

"Listen to him! He's only kidding," said Mr Lazarus admiringly. "Okko's the biggest man in this business. He was the son of the original Wild Man from Borneo – "

"Grandson," growled Okko. "My grandfather invented the business. The only difference is, he was supposed to come from Java and I come from Rikitiki, where I live in the branches of the tall trees eating nuts," he recited rapidly, "undistinguished by the ignorant peasantry from the furry denizens of the woods. I was captured in my infancy by Dikiditchi, the celebrated Russian explorer, who spent three years in the impenetrable jungles and malaria-stricken swamps in his endeavour to secure for Europe the first authenticated link between the lower animals and that cultured product of civilisation – Man!"

"Do you hear him?" asked Lazarus in an ecstasy. "Got the patter and everything! Now, Okko, do me a turn and accept this engagement. It's only for a week, and twenty-five pounds – "

"Twenty-five pounds?" screamed Okko ferociously. "I wouldn't do it under forty!"

"Book him." Alan Stewart closed the deal promptly, and Okko put his signature to the letter in which he agreed, for the sum of forty pounds per week plus the revenue acquired from the sale of his picture post-cards, plus two hours' rest per diem, and a three-course lunch with beer, to appear in the window of Messrs Maber & Maber. Alan Stewart went back to tell Barbara what he had done.

"You'd better explain to those girls downstairs that Okko is a perfectly harmless individual, with a wife and a family, and that he spends his spare time knitting jumpers."

This information was immediately conveyed to the interested staff, and Barbara pushed forward the preparation of the window. A signwriter was called in, a scene-painter made a hurried but effective background representing a primeval forest, and above the window appeared the announcement that on the morrow would appear in the window "Okko, the Great and Original Wild Man from Borneo, captured after three years' continuous hunting by that great Russian scientist, Professor Dikiditchi."

Mr Atterman walked across the road to read the announcement over the heads of the crowd, shook his head and went back.

"That's vulgar, if ever there was vulgarity," he said. "Mabers must have gone mad. Where's Minkey?"

Mr Minkey, weary-eyed and exhausted, dragged himself from his chair to answer the summons. He had been up all night, and he was aching for the comfort of a soft pillow and solitude.

"What's our display this week, Minkey?"

"A girl working a hand-loom," said Minkey.

"A girl working a hand-loom," sneered his employer. "What kind of attraction is that? You've allowed this woman to get ahead of you again! There'll be a crowd in front of her shop tomorrow that'll hold up the road traffic."

"What is she getting?" growled the more dead than alive wire.

"The Wild Man from Borneo. It's an old stunt, but they love old stunts in London. Why couldn't you think of that, you poor boob? Now rustle something for tomorrow."

That afternoon a stout constable came up to Barbara's bureau, stopped for a moment and asked PC Albuera how George was, and, receiving a comforting assurance, came helmetless to the desk and handed Barbara a paper.

"It's a summons, miss, for obstruction," he said, beamed as though it was the greatest joke in the world, and went out to consult Mr Albuera as to whether he thought Harry would ever come back to duty, or was the rheumatism permanent. They had friends in common, it seemed.

Her staff were fagged, ready to drop. Barbara gave orders that the store was to be closed at five instead of six, and notices to this effect were hastily written and exhibited in every department.

"All the earth will be here after the models tomorrow," she told Mr Lark. "I want everybody to be bright and fresh when the doors open."

The money received up to three o'clock had been banked. By the time Maber & Maber turned its unwilling customers into the street another vast sum had accumulated. It was eight o'clock before the money was finally counted and put in the safe.

There remained advertisement proofs to be passed; yet, though she had spent fourteen of the most strenuous hours of her life, Barbara was fresh and wakeful when she at last reached Doughty Street, attended by the faithful Alan.

"If Maber doesn't give you a partnership after this," said Alan when they parted, "he's a slug! You've put fifty per cent on to the value of the business – by the end of this week they'll be offering you a quarter of a million. Lord!" he said enthusiastically, "for two pins I'd leave the advertising business, and you and I would start a store that'd knock 'em dead!"

"If you propose to me, I shall change my agent," warned Barbara, and left him without the power of retort.

She went to bed early, but could not sleep. At the back of her mind were two troubles, one of which centred round Mr Maber's bag and the other those neat little parcels of money stacked at the back of the safe. What a haul for a burglar! she thought, and decided to increase the number of night watchmen, being by no means sure of the energy and enterprise of the elderly gentleman who had slept for forty-nine years in his capacity of night watchman for Maber & Maber.

She lay wide awake, staring into the darkness, and at last she could endure her restlessness no longer and, getting up, turned on the lights. From rising to dressing was but a step. The snores of Myrtle came from the little back room, and without disturbing her servitor Barbara crept down the stairs and hurried into Theobald's Road in search of a taxi.

No two more unwilling burglars ever set forth on their mission of profit and discover than Mr Julius Colesberg and the weary and reluctant assistant.

"It is a pretty ticklish job, Atterman," he complained. "I mean it puts me in a wholly false position. Suppose the night watchman – "

"Suppose nothing," said Mr Atterman, who wasn't running a risk, anyway. He dug his elbow into Mr Minkey's back, and the Live Wire, who was sleeping on his feet, blinked himself awake. "Go and get that bag," said Mr Atterman imperiously, and the two men went forth.

A taxi set them down within a block of Mabers, and after five minutes' delay, during which time, by the united efforts of Julius and the cabman, Mr Minkey was shaken into semi-consciousness, they made for the store.

The staff entrance was in Lawton Street, at the back of the shop, and at this hour, when even Marlborough Avenue was deserted, Lawton Street was a place of the dead. A church bell struck two as Julius, with a trembling hand, fitted the pass-key in the lock. He opened the door stealthily. A light burnt in the passage and in the night watchman's little office.

Julius went suddenly pale, and his heart thumped painfully. The watchman was in his cubby-hole! He sat before a table, his arms outstretched, his head rested ungracefully on his elbow, and he was emitting sounds which could be heard through the glass partition.

"He's asleep," whispered Julius hoarsely.

"Good luck to him!" murmured Mr Minkey, who was swaying to and fro.

Julius gripped his arm, and they tiptoed past where the watchman was watching and up a short flight of stone stairs which brought them to the ground floor level. Thereafter all was plane sailing, and though Mr Minkey, in his extreme languor, stumbled once or twice, they reached the office floor without mishap.

"You stay here," whispered Julius, opening the door of Mr Lark's office. "At the first sound let me know."

"Uh huh!" said the Live Wire, and lowered himself with a joyous sigh into the armchair which Mr Lark reserved for the most favoured callers.

"If you hear any sound, you'll let me know?"

"Uh huh!" said the Live Wire again.

Julius crept along the passage, taking from his pocket the electric torch he had brought. He shook at every sound, and when a floor-board creaked under his tread he jumped. He was perspiring coldly; his heart was in his dry mouth; but, setting his teeth, he moved stealthily to the safe, glided his key into the lock, and in another second the safe swung open.

The first objects revealed by his flash-lamp were the piles of Treasury notes laid against the back of the safe, and at the sight of them he was filled with cold horror. Suppose somebody came and found him in this position – robbing the safe! There would be no other excuse for his presence and the open door.

He saw the bag and, lifting it with a trembling hand, pushed home the door until he heard the lock catch, and went softly out of the office. He had put one foot on the passage carpet when he heard a voice – Barbara's!

She was expostulating with somebody, and he leaned against the panelling, faint and ill. Barbara was waking the night watchman!

What should he do? He was concerned mainly with his own safety, forgot all about the faithful watchdog, sitting with closed eyes in Mr Lark's office. He heard a foot on the stone steps below and made a frantic dive for his old room.

The door was open and he stepped quietly in. Only then was he conscious of the fact that he was carrying Mr Maber's bag.

She was coming up the stairs; there was a heavy, masculine foot behind her. The night watchman was old but wiry. And then, to his horror, he heard a third voice – Lark's.

"It's funny that the same thought struck us both, Miss Storr. I couldn't sleep thinking of that money. And really, Simmonds, I'm surprised at you; you'll have to pull up your socks, my lad, or there'll be a new face in that watchman's box."

"It's the first time I've dozed off for forty-three years," protested the watchman.

"It's the first time you've woke in forty-three years, if you ask me," said Mr Lark.

Julius Colesberg's hair almost stood up. Suppose Lark went into his office; he would find the Live Wire. How was he to escape, hampered by this bag? He thought of the window and opened it gently. Looking out, he saw a man standing on the sidewalk and drew back quickly. And then a low whistle called him and, looking down, he recognised Atterman.

"That you, Julius?" he hissed.

Julius was nodding like an ape.

"Can you get me down? They're here," he whispered as loudly as he dared. "Storr — "

"Give me the bag," demanded Atterman urgently.

Nothing loath, Julius held it out of the window for a second, then dropped it and heard an "Ouch!" He crept to the door and listened. Barbara and her party were coming back from her office, talking excitedly. He heard the word "safe," and his skin crept. Nearer and nearer they came, and then, seized with a sudden inspiration, he put in his pass-key and locked his door on the inside. So doing, he made a noise.

"Who's there?" It was Barbara shaking at the handle.

Mr Colesberg very naturally made no reply. He darted to the window, swung his legs over the sill, and dropped. As he struck the pavement he fell, but was on his feet again in a second. And then somebody gripped him by the arm, and a deep voice, vibrant with satisfaction, said:

"Gotcher!" and he looked into the face of a large and fearsome policeman.

6

For a second Julius was paralysed with fright, and then, wrenching himself free, he ran blindly along the street, with the sound of his pursuer's feet in his ears. He heard a police whistle blow; a man darted across the road to intercept him. Julius dodged down a side street into Brook Street, found himself facing the railings of Hyde Park, and with a superhuman effort leapt to the top of the rails, dragged himself over, and in a second was racing through the darkness to safety.

At four o'clock in the morning a grimy-looking man, with his knees showing through great gaps in his trousers, collarless, smothered with dust and grime, crawled up the steps of Mr Atterman's house in Regent's Park. Tiny leaves hung to his coat by the cobwebs he had disturbed in crawling through bushes to avoid the park police. He had lost his hat, and his usually sleek hair hung all ways over his forehead, giving him a particularly sinister appearance.

Mr Atterman came quickly to the door to answer his gentle knock and admit him.

"Why, for the Lord's sake!" he said, staring in amazement at his tool.

"Give me a drink!" gasped Julius, and staggered into Atterman's sanctum.

"What happened?"

"Did you get the bag?"

"Sure I got the bag." Atterman pointed. It was on a settee under a rug. "It's a good job for me that I saw that policeman coming and got away," he said heartlessly. "I suppose he caught you?"

Julius nodded, and there was a long silence whilst he slaked his thirst. Then Atterman asked:

"Where's Minkey?"

"Minkey?" Julius stared in horror. He had forgotten all about Minkey. "You did say Minkey, didn't you?"

"What else?" said the other impatiently. "Where is he?"

Julius scratched his nose.

"I don't know," he said truthfully. "I left him in Lark's room. If he heard them coming, the coast was clear and he could have got away." He looked thoughtfully at his employer. "He was very sleepy," he said significantly, and Mr Atterman drew a long breath.

"That poor gink didn't fall asleep – he wasn't caught, was he?" he asked, with the first sign of anxiety he had displayed.

"I should imagine it's very likely," said Julius brutally. "By this time he has spilt the porridge, or the beans, or whatever it is you spill."

"For the Lord's sake!" said Mr Atterman under his breath. Then, after long and painful meditation: "He wouldn't talk – he couldn't, anyway," he said. "I was crazy to let him go – he was nearly asleep before he left the house. Have you got the key for this?"

He rose, threw off the covering rug and exposed Mr Maber's bag. Julius shook his head.

"No, but any key will unlock that kind of bag."

"No key that I have will open it. It's a patent lock."

"Cut the side out," suggested Julius helpfully, but here Mr Atterman hesitated. There might be an excuse for Julius retrieving the grip; there was no excuse for opening it forcibly. And the more he thought of it, the less advisable did it seem to take such a step. After all, this bag contained nothing more interesting than a change of clothes. Unless there was also concealed a definite clue as to Mr Maber's present whereabouts, the adventure was not justified, and at this hour seemed a little stupid.

"I'll get out my car and drive you home, Colesberg. The first thing you ought to do is to burn those clothes, so that if there's any kick coming you won't be giving the police any more clues than they've already got."

Julius shuddered.

"And throw away the key of the safe…"

The key of the safe! Julius Colesberg's fingers went like lightening from one pocket to another, and as he searched his face lengthened.

"I've left it in the keyhole," he said, "and it has my name on it!"

"No, miss," said Mr Lark, running his finger from bundle to bundle, "there's no money missing, so far as I can remember."

"Only the bag," said Barbara thoughtfully. "It was – er – " she hesitated – "Mr Maber's bag."

"Did it have any money in it, miss?" asked Lark.

"N-no," she said slowly, "only a little change – I mean, of clothes."

She hurried to remove any impression that at this hour, three o'clock in the morning, she was indulging in ill-timed levity.

"He escaped through the window of Mr Colesberg's room," said Lark. "I've always thought that would be the way a burglar would come in."

"The police haven't caught him?"

"No, miss, but they will," said Lark confidently.

A light was in the eastern sky; day was dawning upon a quiet and silent world. The sensible thing to do would be to make her way home and go to bed, but Barbara never felt less like sleeping.

There was a kitchen and a canteen attached to the establishment, but the cook's staff did not come on duty until eight o'clock. Mr Lark, however, knew his way into larders and produced steaming hot coffee and biscuits, which were gratefully accepted. They breakfasted together in Barbara's room.

"Don't you ever sleep?" she asked curiously.

"Two or three hours a day," said Mr Lark, with airy indifference. "I can sleep anywhere, anyhow, any time. Napoleon was like that, by all accounts."

"So were Wellington and George Washington," she encouraged him.

"Washington – the sewing-machine man?"

She explained gently that Washington was the liveliest of all the wires that ever shocked tyranny. Mr Lark, who was one of those men who never stopped learning, listened with respectful interest; and naturally the subject of Mr Minkey obtruded into the conversation.

"I doubt if he's all he's cracked up to be," said Mr Lark frankly. "I used to have a high respect for him, but I've come now so that I don't think he's any better – well, it's a boastful thing to say, but – "

"Oh, Mr Lark, you're ever so much more of a live wire than he is!" she said.

"Do you think so, miss?" Mr Lark's thumbs strayed to the armholes of his waistcoat.

"Ever so much more. I can't imagine Mr Minkey doing a quarter of what you've done."

"I'll say this for myself," said Mr Lark, who was prepared on any excuse to speak charitably of his own virtues, "that in an emergency I take a bit of beating. I dare say you used to think I was a dry old stick."

Barbara gave him smirk for smirk.

"And I'm sure you thought I was an impossible young female."

Mr Lark protested. He kept a diary, it appeared, and his first impression of Miss Barbara Storr had been distinctly flattering.

"And I'll prove it to you," he said.

He rose, went pattering down the passage; she heard the handle of his door turn and his throaty squeal. A long silence.

"Is anything wrong?" She stood at the door.

"Nothing, miss." He came back to her, looking rather white.

"But of a shock, that's all. Who do you think's in my office?"

She shook her head.

"The Live Wire."

"The what?" she said, not quite believing the evidence of her ears.

"The Live Wire," asseverated Mr Lark solemnly. "Asleep, or drunk, or both."

She went back with him to the room, and Mr Lark switched on the lights. It was true. There was the Live Wire, a huddled, limp figure in an armchair, his mouth wide open, his eyes half closed. He was not a pretty sight.

"Here, wake up," said Mr Lark sternly, and shook the sleeper. "Come on, Wire – live!"

Barbara really thought that was funny. So did Mr Lark. He had to stop to laugh. It wasn't so funny when he had repeated it three times, but as a jest it had its points.

Minkey opened his eyes and stared up.

"Take overhead charges," he said drowsily.

"Come on, wake up – you and your overhead charges! Do you know where you are? You're in the wrong shop. Good Lord! he was the burglar!"

"He wasn't the burglar. I know who the burglar was," she said grimly. "Wake him up, Mr Lark – sing to him."

Mr Lark smiled politely. He didn't think that was very funny, because, as a matter of fact, he had a voice. He was one of those thin-necked men with a prominent Adam's apple, and that kind of people can hardly help singing.

"Wake up, Minkey."

Mr Minkey had fallen asleep again, and was only aroused by the most energetic efforts on the part of his host.

"Take silks," he said. "After you've paid the *ad valorem* duty and overhead – "

"I'm afraid you'll have to let him sleep," said Barbara, as he grunted himself to unconsciousness.

Mr Lark extinguished the light and they went again to Barbara's room.

"Well, if that doesn't beat the band!" said Lark in wonder. "Can you imagine anything—Dear, dear, dear! How did he get there?"

His brows corrugated in thought. He was settling in his mind very important question of honour. Obviously this man should be handed over to the police, but was it done? Did one Live Wire charge another? Or was there not some freemasonry between them? He wished he knew a little more about the etiquette of these things.

"He's probably mistaken the shop and strayed in here – Dozing Daniel wouldn't have noticed him." She referred disrespectfully to the night watchman.

Barbara made a shrewd guess as to the reason for the man's presence.

"Let him sleep. He probably won't wake till this afternoon."

Lark had evidently not exaggerated when he said he could sleep anywhere and anyhow. He went up to the warehouse, threw himself on a pile of genuine Teheran praying mats which had arrived from Birmingham that day, and fell into a dreamless slumber; yet was awake and active when the cleaners arrived at seven o'clock.

The first post was delivered at half-past, and she went quickly through the letters until she came to one addressed in an illiterate hand to "Mr Alling Stuart, c/o Mabers." Alan had warned her that she might expect to hear from Okko that morning, and she had no compunction in opening the letter. A glance at the signature told her that Okko was the correspondent.

Dear Sir (said the letter), – *Having given the matter thort and talked it over with brother artists, must decline kind offer re wild man act, the same being, as everybody says, very lowering to my position.*

Yours truly,
Okko.

Barbara said something naughty. Alan had sent paragraphs to all the newspapers about the wild man.

She heard Mr Lark in the shop below giving instructions to the cleaners (he was so constituted that he could never pass a subordinate without giving some sort of instructions more or less uncalled for), and beckoned him from the head of the stairs.

She showed him the letter.

"This is the wild man you were talking about? That's very unfortunate – very. It was in the evening papers last night; I heard people talking about it going home in the Tube."

"Of course," said Barbara – she did not meet his eyes and her voice was a little husky, but that might have been from tiredness – "it might be possible to get a substitute."

Lark shook his head.

"Not for a wild man, miss. For a salesman or a young lady in the mantle department, but not a wild man from Borneo. I don't suppose he's any more from Borneo than I am."

"If it were possible to get a substitute – " she said, gazing abstractedly down the stairs. "After all, he'd no right to be here. I'm not so sure we couldn't charge him with burglary."

Mr Lark staggered back a pace and held on to a partition.

"Not – not the Wire?" he asked hollowly.

She nodded deliberately.

"He'd be much more comfortable there, if we put a nice mat for him to lie on and covered him with some blankets, than he is in your chair."

Mr Lark opened the door to his room and peeped in. The Wire did not move, though the intruder pushed a chair across the floor. He came back to Barbara.

"Go into your room, miss," he said gently. "I'll tell you when its all over."

There was no word in the early edition about the burglary at Maber & Mabers. Mr Atterman sent specially down to the City for the first papers, examined all the news that came though on the tape, and experienced a genuine relief when he found the item he expected and dreaded did not appear in print.

But what had happened to Minkey? He had got away and gone home probably. The man was exhausted. Musing down on the crowd before Mabers, Eh realised that the "display" was a success. They had got their wild man from Borneo, and evidently he was a fascinating wild man; for even the mounted police patrols were called from the roadway to ride along the pavement and clear the block that was disorganising the traffic. The aid afforded by a pair of powerful field-glasses failed to help him see through the heads that moved and swayed between Mr Atterman and the jungle window; and at last, his curiosity piqued, he went downstairs, crossed the road, and slowly made a progress through the press of people about the window, which was quite distinct from the bulging queues that lined up at the doors.

By dint of patience and perseverance he reached the second rank of the sightseers, and finally, getting an opening, he pushed through. For a moment he could not take in the hideous sight. Stretched upon a new mattress lay a figure, deep in slumber, open-mouthed, altogether hideous.

"Minkey!"

With a strangled cry of wrath, Mr Atterman fought his way clear of the crowd and dashed for the door of Mabers. A policeman caught him and gently pushed him back.

"You've got to take your turn the same as the other ladies, sir," he said. "You needn't worry; there'll be plenty of longery left for you."

"I want to see Miss Storr!" spluttered Atterman.

"I'm sorry, I can't let you in. You've got to join the queue at the end."

But before he had finished, Atterman was flying down the side street to the staff door. The time-keeper saw him, and whilst he was deciding in his mind whether he should ask the business of such an eminent and well-known tradesman, Mr Atterman had brushed past him. He knew roughly the topography of the place, flew up the stone steps and found himself in the shop.

Which was the window? At last he saw it, and went at a run to the little door behind which the unconscious Live Wire was taking out his arrears of rest.

"Excuse me, sir." A commissionaire interposed between him and the door. "You can't touch that. The man's not to be disturbed. He wouldn't think nothing of biting you, or me either."

"Let me go!" howled Mr Atterman. "I want him. He's mine!"

"I'm very sorry, sir." The commissionaire's heart must have been very pure, for he had the strength of ten, and held the struggling, half-demented man at arm's length.

Foaming at the mouth, Mr Atterman leapt for the office stairs, and was checked again outside Barbara's room.

"Got an appointment?" Police-Constable Albuera viewed the suspicious character unfavourably.

"I want to see Miss Storr." The words almost strangled him. "I must see Miss Storr at once."

The door was pulled open and Barbara came out.

"Do you want to see me, Mr Atterman?" she asked innocently.

He could only gibber and point to the floor.

"Yes, we have quite a large number of customers this morning," said Barbara, "and thank you for your congratulations."

"My man – my Mr Minkey!" he squeaked.

"Your Mr Minkey? Who is your Mr Minkey? Oh, I remember! Well, what about him?"

"He's in your window – it's a disgrace… I'll have you arrested."

"Don't threaten," murmured Albuera fiercely.

"It can't be your Mr Minkey," cooed Barbara. "It's the wild man we engaged. I don't know how he got into the shop but we found him on our premises this morning – he was sleeping in Mr Lark's room – and naturally we thought he was the Wild Man from Borneo. Who else could it be? Suppose it isn't the man we think it is, but some person who has feloniously broken into the shop in the night, what shall we do with him?"

She was addressing Police-Constable Albuera Sturman.

"Pinch him," said that authority. "You can't go breaking into shops in the middle of the night. That's committing burglary in the eyes of the law."

The reply sobered Mr Atterman.

"There's been some mistake," he said more mildly. "Either my man in his weariness came into the wrong store, or else a low trick has been played upon a respectable and honest official of Atterman Brothers."

"Incorporated," murmured Barbara, and added: "Such mistake is impossible. It might occur if he had a pass-key, or was accompanied by some discharged employee of Maber & Maber who had a key; but to reach Mr Lark's room, where he was found, it would be necessary for him to have made an entry on to these premises with an illegal object. May I add that my safe was opened last night? It contained a large sum of money."

She saw his colour change.

"Nothing was stolen," said Mr Atterman loudly.

"Some property was stolen; the money, so far as we know, is untouched. The burglars and the receiver," she added – Mr Atterman winced – "are, of course, liable to ten years' penal servitude. I have my theories about the burglary, and I hope you won't disturb them. If I thought for one moment that our wild man was your Mr Minkey – "

She shrugged, and glanced with a meaning smile at Albuera. Albuera blew his nose.

"Perhaps I am mistaken," said Atterman with a cough. "I must confess the likeness is remarkable, very remarkable. Not," he added hastily, "that Mr Minkey bears the slightest resemblance in appearance to a wild man of Borneo or from any other old place. But there is just a possibility that that – " He paused, at a loss for an explanation.

"There's a possibility that a wild man of Borneo may look like Mr Minkey?"

"Exactly," he said.

"Now, constable, will you show Mr Atterman the way out? You don't want to buy anything?" she asked.

Mr Atterman did not trust himself to speak.

Maudie Deane had called the previous morning according to instructions and had been sent home again, with the understanding that she should be within reach if she was wanted. She came again at nine, carrying a black instrument case in her hand.

"I think," said Barbara, regarding her acquaintance thoughtfully, "that this is a morning when a little music might soothe the savage breast – or is it beast?"

"Who's the horror you've got in the window? I've never seen anything like him before," asked Maudie. "Gracious! He gave me the creeps!" She shuddered. "I hope you keep him locked up? He was asleep when I saw him."

"He sleeps all summer," said Barbara. "That kind do. Will you make yourself comfortable on the roof? I'll get Mr Lark to take you up and show you how to get there. He promised to have an umbrella put up for you."

"Shall I be seen from the street?" asked the girl, who also had some professional pride.

"No, from nowhere. The farther back you sit from the parapet, the less likely it is that you'll be seen."

"What shall I play?" asked Maudie eagerly.

Barbara considered this, hand on chin.

"I think you'd better start with 'Where Is My Wandering Boy Tonight?' Will you do that?"

Maudie made a note.

"And then you'd better go on to 'The Wild Man from Borneo Has Just Come to Town' – it's an old tune," said Barbara apologetically, "but possibly you know it?"

Maudie nodded, sucked her pencil and made another note.

"Then, I think" – Barbara looked up to the ceiling for inspiration – "you might give him 'Why are You Sleeping, O My Heart?' Do you know that one?"

Maudie said she did; she spoke rather reluctantly.

"There's nothing very soulful about these, dear," she said. "I thought that 'What'll I Do?' would be a good start off."

"How does it go?"

Maudie recited the words with unction.

"Ye-es," agreed Barbara, "but I think I'd keep that till later."

Soon after Maudie's departure to the roof, before the first wail of her artistic efforts turned the faces of the crowd, Barbara received an unwelcome visitor.

"I know you don't want to see me," smiled Mrs Maber as she came into the room, "but really, my dear, I've come to have a long and serious talk with you."

"Long, yes," said Barbara, "but serious – no. Well, the shorter the better."

The spurious Mrs Maber dropped all pretence of geniality and good nature.

"I've just discovered that my poor, dear husband is in quod!" she said briefly.

Even Barbara knew what "quod" was, and her heart went down into her boots.

"Who told you that absurd story?' she asked vaguely.

"Never mind who told me that story. I'm telling you." The temporary Mrs Maber's voice was strident and domineering. "Between you you've got my husband in trouble, and I'm going to make it hot for some of you. You know he's in prison, and you have kept it from me, his own lawful wife. So that's why I'm not to have my money. That's why my dear William is not allowed to pay his lawful wedded wife – in a church – her rightful dues and demands!"

Her anger was not wholly simulated. The last words which her lawful spouse addressed to her were: "If you make a mess of this I'll murder you!"

"You sitting here, living off the fat of the land," she proceeded rapidly, and in her own language, "a-ordering and a-bossing and a-bullying everybody who comes in my dear husband's place, and treating his own wife as though she was the dirt beneath your feet – I won't stand it! Am I to sit here on the doorstep and beg and pray and go on my knees and crawl for money that's rightfully mine, just because my husband's in prison? I'm going to the papers straight away. I'm going to the Home Secretary – " She hesitated a second. There was somewhere else Mr Hammett had told her to go, but she couldn't remember the place. It was Barbara's opportunity.

"There's no need for you to work yourself into a temper, Mrs Maber," she said with some spirit. "I'll help you all I can. It's perfectly true your husband is in prison, through no fault of his own."

The missus sneered.

"But when you ask me for five hundred pounds you're asking for a lot of money. It may not seem much to you, but it's an awful lot to me. And I'm not prepared – "

"You're not prepared!" scoffed the woman, her voice rising in a cadence of scorn. "I'll let you know, young lady, that I'm standing up for my rights. And I'll go straight away to my solicitor this very minute, and he's one of the best solicitors that's ever been known – the well-known and celebrated Mr Hammett – "

"Hammett!"

Mrs Maber had made a mistake. Her husband had not told her to mention his name; at the same time, he had failed to instruct her not to speak of him. She wasn't even sure that Barbara knew of Hammett's existence.

Barbara was laughing, quietly but intensely.

"Oh, you silly woman!" she said. "And I was just going to give you the money!"

"What do you mean?" asked Mrs Hammett, with a sudden fear.

A finger pointed at her.

"I know how this little idea of the secret marriage came into existence. Just wait."

She drew the telephone to her and gave a number. She was rapidly turning over the counterfoils of the cheque-book.

"Is that the Southern Bank? Miss Storr speaking. Stop payment of DH. 187475…thank you. It hasn't been presented?… Thank you."

Mrs Hammet went a dirty white.

"What's the game?" she asked. Barbara pointed to the door.

"Skip," she said. Barbara on occasions could be almost vulgar.

Mrs Hammett towered over her.

"If I skip, there's going to be trouble – I'm telling you straight. The old man's in quod and you're trying to hush it up. What would it be worth to people like – " She thought for a moment, and only by accident mentioned Atterman. It was a shrewd, if unintentional, reference on her part. "I'm going to tell you something," said Mrs Hammett. "My husband's got to get out of the country, and he's got to get out pretty quick. We're up to our eyes in debt, and he'll be in Brixton Prison next week unless we can clear away out of the country. Our passport is fixed and we're jumping to Canada. Now listen, young miss. I can't get any more for blackmailing you twice than for blackmailing you once, and I don't want to blackmail you at all. But unless you pay up a reasonable sum I'm going over to Attermans, and I'm going to tell him that Maber's in jail."

Barbara sat bolt upright in her chair, watching the woman's face. There was no doubt she was in earnest, that even the threat of prosecution would not turn her from her purpose. To have her arrested would be merely to expose the thing she was trying to hide. In a way, things could not have worked out better than for Hammett to leave that country for good. He was the one man who knew all about the unfortunate episode of Mr Maber's, the one man who could extract an annual toll as the price of silence.

Barbara was eminently practical. She took up the cheque-book, wrote a cheque payable to herself for two hundred pounds, and rang the bell. Then she opened the safe and took out two packages of a hundred pounds and put them on the table, replacing the cheque.

"There's your money, and thank you for your frankness. If you're in England in a week I'm going to jail you."

She opened the door and Mr Maber's temporary wife passed out, if not jubilant, at least satisfied.

That morning Atterman held a council of war, Julius being the other councillor present. The crowd still surged before the window where the sleeping beauty lay at ease, and every time Mr Atterman moved near the window and saw the shocking sight he grew livid of face and incoherent of speech.

'She knows it was you all right," he growled. "Of course she knows. Gosh! You got me into a mess!"

"I?" said the indignant Julius. "What have I done? I wouldn't have gone to the beastly place, only you insisted. And why send me with a dead man, anyway?"

Atterman strode up and down the room, his head between his hands.

"If I could only get one back on her," he said, "only one!... What's that?"

It was the note of a cornet, beautifully clear and sweet. Mr Atterman's knees trembled. There was only one person in the world who could make a cornet talk that way. He looked round for some sign of her, but the sun glinted on no brazen mouth. It seemed almost as if the melody came from the sky. For a second Mr Atterman, who had a leaning towards spiritualism, wondered if Maudie was dead. And then he recognised the tune and ground his teeth.

"She doesn't know what she's doing," he said. "That fiend of a woman has put her up to it…taunting me! Where the devil is she?"

He searched the street, the facia of Mabers', and the sky, and presently located the sound.

"She's on the roof," he said, dashed out of the room, rang furiously for the elevator, and was carried up to his own roof.

Yes, there she was, a pathetic figure, making music for his embarrassment. He waved his hand in a signal, but Maudie played best with her eyes shut.

"The Wild Man from Borneo" was being blared forth. The vulgarity of it! And Maudie was such an artist.

Mr Atterman went back to his office, his heart filled with hate for the girl who had flaunted him.

"I'm going to see what's in that bag," he said. "I don't care what happens. We'll go back to the house and you cut it open."

"*You* cut it open," suggested Julius. "I've done enough cutting and climbing to last me for the rest of my life."

"Does it matter who does it?"

Mr Colesberg pondered the point.

"I don't know. I'll ask Peeker."

"Who is Peeker?" demanded Julius.

Mr Atterman pushed a bell.

Of all the shop detectives in the world, Peeker was perhaps the most scientific. Peeker's task at Attermans was to distinguish the kleptomania of wealthy customers from the thieving propensities of the lower orders. He was a terror to all shoplifters, professional and amateur; his gimlet eyes penetrated pillow muffs wherein illicit lace and stockings were concealed; he saw though capacious bags into which odds and end of ribbons had been dropped.

But he was something more than a shop detective. Nobody seeing this short, stout man with the rosy, open face and the curly hair would have suspected that he harboured within his soul an ambition to greater things.

He despised himself for the pettiness of his occupation, and bitterly regretted the lack of inches that had debarred him from entry to the police and the attainment of an assured and honoured position at Scotland Yard.

In the bicycle shed at the back of his house in Camden Town he maintained a notable laboratory. Here were the microscopes and rows of bottles, stills and Bunsen burners with which he occupied his spare time. He had read every informing book on crime and the criminal that was procurable. He had read Lombroso, Mategazza and the *Anthropological Review*. He could distinguish mammalian blood from egg-stains, and could detect arsenic (to which he referred by its nickname $As^2 O^2$) by the three recognised tests. To such a man the petty nature of his daily task was both irksome and humiliating. He was something of an authority on criminal law.

He came and stared gravely before his employer, twisting his watch-guard.

"Peeker, suppose I have in my possession a bag, the property of somebody else, which I have reason to believe contains information which I ought to have – "

"And which is wrongfully withheld from you?" asked Peeker.

"Yes," said Atterman, jumping at this interpretation.

"Stolen property?"

"Um – yes, it might be for all that I know to the contrary."

"Open it," said the oracle simply, and waited. "Is that all sir?"

"That is all, Peeker."

Mr Peeker withdrew.

"There you are," said Atterman. "He knows!"

The storekeeper had got past any nice feelings that he might have had. He was prepared not only to cut the bag but to commit an even more desperate crime to get even with this unwomanly creature.

He at first intended waiting till lunch-time, but the maddening repetition of significant tunes made work impossible, and collecting Julius from the little room in which he had been installed, he telephoned for his car and they drove back to Regent's Park.

The bag was in a cupboard, and Atterman, taking it out, placed it on the table.

"Shut the doors and lock 'em," he said quietly.

He took from his pocket a knife that he had collected from his bargain basement – one of those never-wear-out-able articles which are so popular with the junior boyhood of our country.

"Now," he said, and stuck the knife through the upper part of the bulging hide and drew. The knife broke.

"There is another blade," suggested Julius softly.

Mr Atterman opened the second blade and again stabbed the leather, and again the knife broke.

"Have you got a razor?" asked Julius after he had turned out his own pockets to prove that he himself carried no weapon of any kind.

"I have several razors," said Mr Atterman coldly.

"Try one that you didn't get at Attermans," said the rude Julius.

Mr Atterman went upstairs and returned with a large, white-handled, bright-bladed weapon, and this time went more cautiously to work. He had first to cut through the hide and then through the lining. When he had finished, a jumble of stained clothes was revealed.

"What on earth are these? This isn't a change!"

He pulled out a pair of trousers: they were muddy from the ankles to the knees; one leg was slightly slit at the seam; they were even mud-stained elsewhere.

"He's been sitting in the road, or fallen," suggested Julius. "That's queer."

Again Atterman dipped into the unlucky bag and pulled out a shirt and a dress jacket. The jacket was split at the collar, and there were signs here of a struggle. The elbows were torn, the cuffs covered with some sinister-looking stains. Julius watched open-mouthed, incapable of speech, and then Mr Atterman spread out the shirt. The bosom was muddy, and something worse. Great bloodstains stretched from the shoulder to the second buttonhole.

"My God!" breathed Atterman, his hands shaking.

Without another word, he took up the telephone and, providentially remembering the number, called his store.

"Mr Atterman speaking. Tell Mr Peeker I want him." He waited, talking over his shoulder. "We've got to go carefully to work here," he said in a muffled voice. "I don't want to bring in the police until I've had Peeker – Is that you, Peeker? Mr Atterman speaking. Come right away up to my house – a murder has been committed!"

He put down the telephone and faced the late junior partner.

"The question is," said Mr Atterman slowly, "where has she hidden the body?"

7

Mr Maber was murdered; they had no doubt on the subject. Here was the damning proof. Even Mr Atterman shuddered at the sight of those tell-tale stains – the pale pink stain on the left, the brown bloodstain on the right of the shirt bosom.

"That looks like wine," said Julius, indicating the pink discoloration.

Mr Atterman nodded dejectedly.

"She probably lured him on – with wine," he said. "Young in years and old in wickedness. What a curse money is!"

Julius agreed. Other people having money was the most cursed thing he knew.

"I liked him," said Mr Atterman softly. "There was something about the poor old boy that was very, very – " He stopped, at a loss for a word, but Julius offered no suggestion. "He had that peculiar charm," said Mr Atterman, "which you might describe as – " He waited for Mr Colesberg's help.

"Exactly," said Julius. "I have often thought that."

"Such men," said Mr Atterman, "for all their – what is the word? – have a side to them which is – "

"I have felt that," said Julius quietly, "with him especially."

He sighed.

"I suppose he died intestate. These good-natured, careless old gentlemen, they seldom make provision – although," as a thought occurred to him, "he was not without gratitude. I remember his saying to me once, 'Colesberg, I'm greatly obliged to you.' It was some little service I'd rendered," said Julius modestly. "I gave up my taxi to him one rainy day – a mere nothing. But these little things count in the minds of the lonely, brooding kind of man."

Mr Atterman nodded.

"I shall hate the publicity of it," he said, "although publicity of any kind is very good for business. As for the girl – " He shrugged his shoulders.

"It seems a pity," said Julius, "and yet the law's the law."

They sat and gloomed on the virtues of the departed Mr Maber, on the queer and romantic drama of his death; they speculated, having a limited knowledge of such things, upon the disposal of his remains, until Mr Atterman's servant entered to announce Mr Peeker. The sleuth-hound of Attermans preserved an impassive mien.

"Murder, I understand?" he said without emotion. He might have been asking the time.

He listened, almost in complete silence, to the story of the discovery, examined the shirt, the trousers and the coat.

"That is undoubtedly blood," he said, examining the shirt, "and this is unquestionably mud."

Absent-mindedly he took one of Mr Atterman's priceless coronas from a box, bit off the end, and accepted a light which Julius offered to him with a curt nod of thanks.

"The coat has been torn in a struggle," he said. "If you were to reconstruct the crime you would say that he was grasped by the collar thus" – he caught Julius by the throat in a grip of iron; Mr Colesberg's face went a deep purple – "and he was struck on the head…no, that couldn't be. I'll try with my right hand."

"Just tell us what happened – there's no need to demonstrate," begged Julius, recovering his breath.

"He was held by the right hand and struck with the left. That is why the blood is on the right-hand side. A champagne bottle – the wine-stains suggest that."

"Champagne is yellow, not red," said Mr Atterman.

"Some champagnes turn red on exposure to the air," explained Mr Peeker quietly. "I should say that he was pulled down in the open – the woman had a confederate. A tall, dark man – "

"How do you know?" demanded Atterman, startled.

Peeker did not enlighten him. He pictured the assailant as a tall, dark man. A short, fair assassin would have been incongruous.

"The body was then dragged some distance – probably into a disused outhouse."

He was examining the pair of patent-leather shoes that the others had overlooked.

"Scratches here," he pointed. "Somebody stood on his foot – the leather is cracked."

He put his hand into the inside breast pocket of the dress coat and drew out two green slips.

"She took him to the Empire Theatre."

He searched the other pocket and made his most important discovery. It was a piece of crumpled card, torn apparently from a wine list, for on one side was printed the price of liquors. The note was written shakily in pencil.

Dear Barbara – For heaven's sake, do not tell a soul…

Here the writing ended.

"Evidently she knew something about him," said Peeker piecing together the story. "She threatened to expose him – demanded her price, and on his refusal – " He shrugged.

"This is a matter for the police – " began Atterman.

"Wait." Peeker raised a warning hand. "Don't let us bring in those bunglers. The man may still be alive!"

Atterman breathed more quickly.

"You mean – ?"

"There are a score of dens where he may be hidden. I know places that are beyond your wildest dreams. To bring in the police may mean his death! Dead men," said Mr Peeker, "tell no tales."

"What are we to do?" asked Julius, all of a flutter.

"Leave everything to me." Peeker took out a notebook. "What is this girl's private address? Where is she to be found? Mr Maber's private address?"

He finished writing and closed his book.

"The thing is clear," he said. "The girl is in difficulties—probably in the hands of money-lenders. In her desperation she persuades the old man to take her to dinner, and after to a theatre, where the confederate is picked up. On some excuse – probably to drop the third man – they drive to some lonely party of town. Maber gets out, there is a struggle, and he is struck down and dragged to a cellar. The girl, wishing to spirit him away to the country where he will be away from prying eyes, gets a change of clothing – evening dress would be conspicuous. She drugs him – the rest is easy."

"What is the rest?" asked Julius.

Mr Peeker shrugged again.

"Leave this to me. In twenty-four hours you may call in the police. In forty-eight hours these two people will be under lock and key. You didn't want to see me about anything else, Mr Atterman?"

He gave the impression that it was hardly worth while bringing him to Regent's Park to discuss a mere murder.

8

There were two other people holding strong views on the iniquity of Barbara Storr. Mr and Mrs Hammett did not go to Canada, did not leave for the Continent, did no more, in fact, than pay the most pressing of their creditors, and the change of plans was due to two causes. In the first place, the gentleman who had agreed to purchase the lawyer's furniture at a knock-out price had demanded at the eleventh hour to be shown a receipt for the same; an embarrassing request, inasmuch as the prettily furnished apartment rented by Mr Hammett had been garnished on what is known as the hire-purchase system, whereby, for a seemingly inadequate sum, a large-hearted and trustful tradesman supplies his client or clients with beds and carpets, dining-room suites of handsome appearance, gorgeous overmantels – in fact, all that a young married couple, or an old married couple for the matter of that, may desire. Having paid the deposit and received the goods, the hirer paid so much a month for years and years, at the end of which time such of the furniture as had not fallen to pieces from old age became his property. Mr Hammett had not paid for years and years, not even for months and months. Accordingly, he was making no great sacrifice when he offered his household goods to a man who had hitherto been a friend.

There was another reason. Amongst the correspondence waiting for him – and this included a very ominous letter from the Law Society – he had found an urgent note from an old client, Captain Griffin of the *Silina*. Mr Hammett had been very useful to the captain: once in a little matter of broaching cargo, and once when he faced the less serious charge, from a seaman's point of view, of assault with intent to murder. In each case Mr Hammett, in his legal wisdom, had discovered certain flaws in the evidence for the prosecution, and the captain had gone scot-free. Thereafter it was the habit of Captain Griffin, whenever he was in London (he was master of a coasting vessel which plied between Leith and Newcastle), or whenever he was in any kind of difficulty, to consult his learned friend, paying for the advice sometimes in cash, sometimes in kind. Many a good case of whisky had gone astray on the passage from Leith to London, and had found its way by some mysterious method into Mr Hammett's buffet.

And just at this moment Hammett was in need of a little advice himself from a man who was familiar with the character and climate of foreign countries. He was not sure that Canada would offer to him the opportunities to which his genius entitled him.

And there was no immediate hurry. That afternoon the shipping agency had refunded the deposit he had paid on his tickets and Mr Hammett was not ill-pleased.

"It will be nearly three weeks before Maber comes out," he said shrewdly, "and we shall never have another chance like this. In that time, if I have the brains of a puff-adder, I should be able to get a cool thousand out of Maber's business. Then we can think about skipping."

"But how are we going to get it?" asked Mrs Hammett, naturally intrigued.

"There are several ways," said Mr Hammett as he knocked off the ash of his cigar into the untidy fireplace. "The only thing is" – he fondled his narrow chin thoughtfully – "could we do a real big bit of business and get away with it?"

"You're clever enough for anything," said Mrs Hammett, one of the few people in the world who admired him.

Mr Hammett did not need to be told that. A very long acquaintance with the lowest form of criminal practice had educated him in the art and artfulness of money-getting. He knew a dozen methods, all effective, all more or less simple – and all invariably fatal to a man's liberty.

There was an imposingly headed letter on the table. He picked it up and read it again. It was a letter from the secretary of the Law Society, calling upon him to appear before the council "at eleven o'clock in the forenoon" on a certain day to explain certain things which, he knew, were inexplicable. That inquiry could only have one end: his disappearance from the honourable roll of officers of the court. He had had many narrow escapes of being "struck off," and in a large degree his very obscurity and unimportance had helped him avoid that unpleasant contingency. But the end of his practice had come; a prosecution might even follow.

Mr Hammett was not distressed, was not even annoyed. What worried him most was the regularity of the means he had in his possession for leaving the country. For his passport was in his own name; an inartistic photograph of himself decorated its pages. The man who is travelling on a passport is easily traced; consular offices find their only recreation in the detection of fugitives.

"I'd do it like a shot," he mused. "Only it is certain they will be after me."

"What about Griffin?" asked Mrs Hammett. "Couldn't he get you away?"

Mr Hammett sneered.

"Don't be a fool. He could get me away from London and Leith, but what use would that be? Captain Griffin!"

"There's him," said Mrs Hammett, and hurried out to admit the visitor.

Captain Griffin was a small and hairy man, with a slight cast in one eye.

"How do you do, Mr Hammett?" He greeted his friend warmly, and he had reason for his affection. "I thought I'd pop in to see you before I went. I've got a bit of law to talk about, if you don't mind, ma'am?"

Mrs Hammett modestly offered to withdraw her presence, but the captain, with that old-world courtesy which is part of the sea tradition, refused to entertain the idea.

"We're all friends here," he said, "and what I tell your legal husband won't be repeated, as I well know."

He drew the chair nearer to the table. Mrs Hammett, like the good hostess she was, produced a black bottle from the sideboard, a jug of water and a siphon of soda, gave the captain permission to smoke – a permission he had already anticipated – and settled herself down, more curious than her husband to hear this point of law discussed.

"I want to know my position," said Captain Griffin slowly, giving two words to one puff of smoke. "Mind you, Mr Hammett, I'm being paid well. Thirty pounds a month and one per cent bonus on the cargo. And there's no risk and no danger. I took supplies on at Leith, and I'm only waiting now for the young gentleman from Glasgow who's going out with us. Now the question is – you know the laws of America – what can I get for it?"

"For what?" asked Mr Hammett, suddenly interested.

"Well, for this rumming, or whatever they call it."

Hammett suddenly sat bolt upright. When he thought at all, he thought quickly.

"You're rum-running?" he asked.

"That's the word. What can I get for it? Some say ten years; some say a fine."

Mr Hammett did not answer immediately.

"When do you leave?" he asked.

"Tomorrow night about eleven o'clock. We're lying in the Pool, and we get out at high tide."

A faint colour had come into Mr Hammett's face. He saw his way clearly now.

"You needn't bother about what you'll get," he said rapidly. "There's very little chance of your being caught. Griffin, how would you like to take me with you?"

"You, sir?" The captain stared at him. "Do you want to go on a voyage?"

Hammett nodded.

"Take you, sir? Why, I'll take you with pleasure. I'd pay money to have a lawyer on the spot; and it'll be a good holiday too. We'll be back in November."

"I don't want any holiday," said Mr Hammett emphatically. "All I want is to be landed in America without anybody knowing." Then, seeing the suspicious look in the captain's eyes, he leaned forward and, confidentially, "It's a secret mission," he said with mystery, "for the Government."

The captain frowned.

"Not about booze?" he asked with a sudden fear.

"Booze?" Hammett shrugged his shoulders. "No, about gold, and certain other things that I'm not going to talk about."

The captain pulled at his beard.

"And your lady?" he asked.

"She'll go by the ordinary steamer." He met his wife's eye coldly. "When I send for her," he added.

The captain sighed his relief.

"We haven't got any accommodation for ladies on my old tub, but you'll be welcome, sir. We sail at eleven. You'd better not come till half-past ten, otherwise you'll be attracting attention. I'll have a boat waiting for you at China Stairs – that's a little narrow turning near the slipway in Wapping. Nobody need see you come on board, and it will be easy to land you. I'll send you off in one of the motor-boats that are coming to meet me outside the limit."

They shook hands on that.

The captain left half an hour later, and Mr Hammett spent the rest of his night perfecting a scheme which had never been known to fail.

The third day of the great sale dawned in hope, for the result of the first two days' trading had been stupendous. And yet Barbara found herself wondering, with a little quaking at heart, what would be Mr Maber's verdict when he discovered the depths to which his house had fallen. After the first days of mad excitement, the inevitable reaction had come, and Barbara had lost a little of her independence and wanted somebody to lean on. In these circumstances it was with a sense of thankfulness that she saw the tall figure of Alan Stewart waiting patiently for her at the corner of the street when she came out in the morning.

"I've got good news for you," he said, as he fell in by her side, "O resurrector of dead businesses! What did Atterman offer for Mabers?"

This was not a moment for reticence, and she told him. He whistled.

"The old skinflint! Well, Tennyson & Burns came to see me last night – Tennyson himself. He knew that I was a little on the inside of things, and he wanted to know whether Maber would take three hundred thousand pounds – half cash and half shares."

"The answer is in the negative," said Barbara promptly.

"I'd think it over," he urged her. "you told me that Maber had left you power to conclude the sale, and if he was willing to take a hundred and twenty thousand – "

"He was willing to take a hundred thousand," she interrupted.

"Well, it would be two hundred per cent more satisfaction for him to take the bigger sum," said Alan. "I had wild ideas of raising the money myself, putting you in as managing director, giving you a big interest, and marrying you – "

"To save the commission? No, thank you," said Barbara with a lift of her chin. "That kind of partnership doesn't appeal to me as much as you would think. Why don't you marry Maudie?"

"Maudie?" He frowned. "Oh, you mean your soloist?"

"My late soloist," said Barbara grimly. "Never trust women in business, Alan – Mr Stewart."

"Alan's better," he said gently. "The Word that Pulls. What is the matter with the horn-blowing female?"

"Maudie's deserted and gone over to the enemy. Mr Lark saw her sneaking in at the side door of Attermans just before we closed, and when I got home I found this extraordinary note from her."

Barbara opened her bag, took out the letter and handed it to her companion.

"Unravel it for me," she said.

Alan read:

Dear Miss Storr,
There are things that I have to be awfully careful about, being a
professional. You cannot touch pitch without being defiled. And papa's
position has to be considered, being near his pension and not a black
mark against him. As you've been so kind to me, and for the sake of
old times, I shall not, of course, breathe a word of the past.

Yours sincerely,
Maud Alice Deane.

"What on earth does she mean?" he asked in astonishment.

"I'd like to know," said Barbara, replacing the letter in her bag. "Anyway, she's gone back to her ridiculous red coat and plumed hat. Atterman is crazy about her still; that is the impression she left with me. He never struck me as a sentimentalist, and who her pa may be, heaven knows."

Once or twice, as they were walking, Alan had looked back over his shoulder.

"I wonder who the dickens he is?" he said.

Behind was a stout, placid man, twirling an umbrella as he walked, a beam of satisfaction on his healthy face, his derby hat at an angle on his head. She half-turned and surveyed the imperturbable stranger.

"Do you know him?"

She shook her head.

"I saw him near the house. I had an idea he was waiting for somebody. He's not following us, is he?"

"Very likely," said Barbara, enjoying the experience. "Probably your wife has employed him."

"Nobody knows better than you that I'm not married," said Alan Stewart hotly; "except," he added, "to my art."

"I never laugh before ten o'clock," said Barbara.

She had expected a diminution of interest in Mabers' extraordinary sale. The best of the bargains had been disposed of on the second day, and the Paris models – such as had not been torn to pieces by infuriated bargainers – were all but exhausted. But Mr Lark, giving another display of his unsuspected gifts for organisation, had cleared a line of silks from Paris, chartered three aeroplanes to bring them across, and had worked the greater part of the night unpacking and pricing. These new bargains Barbara had advertised in some trepidation, for when the advertisement copy had been written the silks were still in Paris. Late the previous night Mr Lark had sent a reassuring message, however, and she arrived at the store to discover the old crowd and the old queues. In the course of the night the display window had been cleared of its jungle trimmings, and was now piled high, inartistically if effectively, with samples of the new purchases.

Barbara had ceased to worry about the missing bag. She did not doubt that it was in the hands of Mr Julius Colesberg and his confederate, and she wondered what conclusions they would draw from their discovery. The only fear that she had was that the truth about Mr Maber's disappearance should be revealed by accident. There must have been people in the court when he was tried and sentenced; one of these might have recognised him, told the story to his near acquaintances, and let loose the trickle which might well become a flood. But nothing of the sort had occurred. The only person who was in any way dangerous had fled the country – she did not regret the hundreds she had paid; that was money well spent. Before the month was up, many things would have happened. She was inclined to consider the new offer for the business, knowing how much Mr Maber detested his occupation. But against this inclination was a desire to present him with a revivified Maber & Mabers, and leave it to his discretion as to what he should do with his new property.

She recognised that she had not so much increased the value of the firm as opened the eyes of those who looked upon it as a decaying concern to its real value. It had always been worth what was now offered, probably a little more.

She was immersed in the day sheets, checking outgoings, totalling profits, examining what Mr Minkey loved to call "overhead," when

Police-Constable Albuera came into the room and closed the door behind him.

"Hammett wants to see you," he said in a low voice.

She jerked herself erect. The shock left her speechless.

"Hammett?" she said incredulously. "You mean solicitor?"

"The snide solicitor," he corrected.

"Are you sure it's he?"

She had pictured Mr Hammett steaming steadily westward, singing songs of joy and triumph.

Albuera nodded.

"Show him in," she said.

It was a different Mr Hammett who came in from the shabby little man she had known. His frock-coat was new and well-fitting, his trousers as new and creased; his silk hat was shiny, his linen spotless; and in his left eye was a gold-rimmed monocle which he had some difficulty maintaining.

"Good morning, Miss Storr," he said briskly, laid a big portfolio on the table, pulled up a chair, placed his hat on a convenient ledge, and opened the portfolio, all with the air and manner of one who had very little time to spare but intended to occupy that space as usefully as possible.

She fixed him with a stern look.

"I'm rather surprised you've come, Mr Hammett," she said.

He smiled sadly and shook his head.

"I can well understand your surprise, Miss Storr," he said. "I intended calling at Scotland Yard on my way, but I thought I had better see you first. This is yours, I think?"

He took from the new portfolio a green and grey strip and laid it on her blotting-pad. She saw at a glance that it was the cheque which she had given to Mrs Hammett, and which she had stopped.

"Yes, that is mine," she said wonderingly. "It is the cheque I gave to your wife – "

He shook his head sadly.

"I have never been married," he said with quiet earnestness. "You have, I regret to say, been the victim of an unscrupulous adventuress — I will not say swindler, because happily I have an unrivalled system of intelligence which enabled me to nip this nefarious plot in the bud."

Barbara was staggered.

"She's not your wife?"

"I have never had a wife," said Mr Hammett. "I have loved, but I have never had a wife." He sighed heavily and lowered his eyes. "The woman I should have married unfortunately — " He shrugged his shoulders, shook his head and coughed, thereby intimating that the love of his life was either dead or married to somebody else. "The woman was in court when Mr Maber was sentenced" (this agreed with Barbara's own fears), "and being a notorious blackmailer, and seeing me talking to you, she hatched the plot."

Barbara took and examined the slip. She saw that a red pen-mark had been run through the signature.

"I did that," said Mr Hammett. "The moment I discovered the plot and wrestled the cheque from this wretched woman, I took the very natural precaution of erasing the signature so that in no circumstances could the cheque be cashed."

"Did you erase the two hundred pounds in cash I gave her?" asked Barbara quietly.

Mr Hammett's eyebrows went up; on his face was a look of horror.

"You gave her two hundred pounds in cash!" He pressed his hand to his forehead. "Miss Storr, how could you be so indiscreet? And I thought that I had saved you from being swindled! Nothing now remains but to go immediately to Scotland Yard," he said, half rising, and thinking better of his intention when he saw she made no attempt to check his departure. "Fortunately I know where I can lay my hands on her, and before" — he looked at his watch — "twelve o'clock she shall be in custody."

He took out a long and narrow book and turned the pages rapidly. She saw they were covered with writing, and from the stamps which appeared at intervals she guessed that they were receipts.

"Meantime, in justice to one," said Mr Hammett, "who occupies a position in a very honourable profession, a very generous profession, and a profession very jealous of the honour of its members, I will ask you to place on record the fact that I have restored the cheque. By two o'clock this afternoon, at the latest, I shall restore as much of her ill-gotten gains as this unscrupulous female has not squandered in riotous living."

He twisted the book round. Barbara saw an entry and read it mechanically:

Received from Mr Cornelius Hammett, MA, LLD solicitor, one cheque given by misrepresentation to Jane Smith alias Margaret Hammett, cheque numbered DH.187475.

"I'll do this certainly," said Barbara, taking her pen.

"On behalf of Maber & Maber – your usual signature," murmured Mr Hammett.

She signed "William Ebenezer Maber, by his attorney, Barbara Storr," in the red-ruled oblong which appeared about all the receipt signatures. Mr Hammett with his own hand blotted the signature, put the book back in his portfolio.

"Now as to the two hundred pounds, I don't think we need have a prosecution. In fact, I think a prosecution is very undesirable in all the circumstances."

Barbara agreed heartily.

"All we want to do is get the money back, and I will secure you that, though I am not so sure that I shall recover every penny. I shall of course charge no fee."

"Do you really and seriously mean that you weren't in this swindle?" asked Barbara bluntly.

A look of pain spread over Mr Hammett's face.

"I regret that such a thought should have been entertained by you for one moment," he said gravely.

The man was hurt; he waggled his head as though to shake down the emotion which rose unbidden, squeezed her hand affectionately and took his departure, nodding pleasantly to the scowling Constable Albuera.

The girl examined the cheque, tore it into small pieces and dropped it in the waste-paper basket. That was the end of an unpleasant adventure. She had wronged the little man, and, heartily relieved to learn that no prosecution was impending, she was in a mood to revise her uncharitable views of him.

Mr Hammett beckoned the first taxi he found and drove straight away to the little office which he alone occupied. He had dispensed with his clerk many years before, and had not even the services of a typist. Locking the door of his room, he took out the receipt book and wetted the edges of the page on which the girl had signed. The top layer of paper was easily removed; it was thin, opaque and added little to the thickness of the page. Beneath was an ink carbon, and beneath that, covered by the wording of the receipt, a blank cheque on the Southern Bank, Marlborough Avenue branch. The ink carbon was of the finest possible texture; the signature of the cheque might have been written by Barbara's pen instead of being, as it was, a carbon copy. He took a big reading-glass, carried the cheque to the light and examined 'William Ebenezer Maber, by his attorney Barbara Storr,' but could not fault it. Carefully covering the signature with a sheet of blotting paper, he filled in the cheque to himself, added in brackets "legal expenses," and this done, replaced the cheque in his portfolio and went out to meet his wife and to give her instructions.

A certain sleuth-hound from a place of vantage had seen Mr Hammett enter the store and had recognised him as a lawyer of dubious character.

Mr Peeker knew his man as the legal adviser of a notorious professional shoplifter of South London, and his presence at Mabers was rather astonishing.

Peeker's office window commanded a view of Barbara's sanctum. He had been watching her all morning through a pair of field-glasses, and now he saw Mr Hammett enter. Unconscious of the fact that she was overlooked, Barbara had drawn the half-curtains, for Mr Maber's office was rather dark, and the watcher witnessed the scene that followed. The passing of the cheque, its destruction…

When Hammett regained the street, the watcher was on his heels. All the time he was in his office Nemesis waited in a taxi by the sidewalk, watching (with some anxiety) the fare click up. When Hammett discended at Pignoli's restaurant at King's Cross, Mr Peeker followed him in and took a place at the next table, where the lawyer's wife had been waiting.

"It is all right," he said in a low voice.

"There won't be any trouble?" she asked anxiously.

"Trouble!" he scoffed. "I've got her like that!" He pressed his thumb on the table with a glance at his neighbour. Mr Peeker was absorbed in his newspaper, and, moreover, when the waiter came for his order, was so deaf that the noble Italian had to shout in his ear.

"The point is," said Hammett more naturally after this revelation, "she's scared of anybody knowing where Maber is – it would be ruin if it came out...it would mean death to a man like that."

Peeker was straining his ears. Barbara Storr would be ruined...it would be death to Maber if anybody knew where he was! He experienced for the first time the joy that comes to the great detective when logic and deduction have led him to the support of concrete facts.

Thereafter, Hammett spoke in a lower tone, and the listener heard little that was helpful, though Mr Hammett was giving instructions to his wife which would have been very illuminating to the eavesdropping shop detective had he overheard them.

At twenty minutes past three, ten minutes before the bank's closing hour, she was to telephone Barbara, representing herself to be the agent of a German wholesaler who had a stock of artificial silks. He had taken the trouble to get prices that morning from wholesalers, and he was able to give a list of prices fifty per cent below the market value.

"Hold her with this for ten minutes. She won't recognise your voice on the phone."

"But what's the idea? You're not trying to sell her these silks?" asked Mrs Hammett, troubled.

Mr Hammett drew a long breath.

"This is not the time to argue," he said, "and not the time for explanation. But as you're more or less brainless, I suppose I'd better tell you that I want you to hold her so that the bank can't get back to her by phone."

At twenty minutes past three that afternoon he presented himself at the bank and pushed the cheque nonchalantly across the counter. The cashier looked up at him and examined him through the grille.

"Are you Mr Hammett?" he said.

"Yes," said the lawyer with a quiet smile.

His heart was beating at an abnormal rate, but he showed no signs of his profound agitation, which increased with every second of the cashier's silence.

"How will you have this?"

Mr Hammett could have swooned with joy.

"Hundreds," he said nonchalantly.

The cashier counted out twenty notes, counted them again, counted them a third time, scribbled his pencil across the signature on the cheque, and pushed the notes under the grille. Mr Hammett left without apparent haste. His taxi was waiting, and three minutes before closing time he walked into the marble hall of the Eighth National Bank of New York, and came out into the street, his pockets bulging with hundred-dollar bills.

Mr Atterman's telephone bell rang and the voice of Peeker spoke urgently.

"I've found the other man," he said.

"The confederate?" asked Mr Atterman quickly.

"He's a man named Hammett. He's blackmailing Storr. Maber's alive, but they've got him a prisoner somewhere."

"Wait," said Mr Atterman, and imparted the information to Julius, who was filling in the time between breakfast and lunch by eating his nails.

"Alive, is he?" Julius did not seem overjoyed. Perhaps the recollection of the service he had rendered the old man and the proverbial gratitude of the aged, which finds expressions in codicils, had slightly shifted his moral outlook.

"I knew that bird Peeker would find him," said Mr Atterman exultantly. "Now, Julius, I guess our plan is clear. If we save Maber's life, he can't help feeling grateful, and I shouldn't be surprised if it didn't make a whole lot of difference to our negotiations. I guess he'll be just the sickest man in the world with that Storr woman. 'Atterman,' he'll say, 'you've been wonderful to me. If it hadn't been for you I should have been a dead man.' "

" 'For you and Colesberg,' " suggested Julius.

"Well, maybe he'll mention you," conceded Mr Atterman. "Anyway, I'll fix it so that he knows you've been sort of interested."

Peeker's voice was calling him impatiently on the phone.

"I can't wait, or those birds will slip me," he said.

"Go right ahead, son," said Mr Atterman genially. "Spare no expense. Report here before six and at Regent's Park after. We'll be in all the time, waiting on you."

It was half-past nine that night before he heard again from his sleuth.

"I'm speaking from Wapping," said the low voice of Mr Peeker. "He's in an eating-house near here, disguised."

"Who – Maber?"

"No, not Maber – Hammett. I've trailed him all day. He's dressed like a rough sailor and wearing a false moustache."

Mr Atterman's eyes lighted.

"Good boy," he said encouragingly, "Let me know…spare no expense…"

Nine, ten, eleven – midnight came before the telephone bell rang again, and then it was not Peeker's, but a deep, official voice that spoke.

"Is that Mr Atterman?"

"Yuh," said Mr Atterman.

"I am Sergeant Johnson of the Thames Police. Have you got a man in your employ named Peeker?"

Atterman turned pale.

"Yes."

"We've found his overcoat by the riverside. One of our constables heard a splash in the water, went down to the river steps, and found the coat half in and half out of the river."

Atterman's head reeled. The house of Maber & Maber had become almost a menace.

9

Julius was staying at Mr Atterman's house and had retired to bed at eleven o'clock. Mr Atterman went up the stairs two at a time, and without knocking at the door dashed in, switched on the light and dragged the startled man to wakefulness.

"She's got Peeker!" he said breathlessly. "You're next!"

"Eh?" said Julius.

"You're next!" Atterman pointed a trembling finger at the horrified man.

"She's got Peeker?" Julius was a picture of horror. "You mean Barbara Storr…got Peeker? What's she doing with him?"

"You fool, she's murdered him!" hissed Atterman.

Julius staggered into the bathroom and drank three glasses of cold water in rapid succession; and following him, Mr Atterman stood at his elbow and gave in detail the story of the crime.

"Peeker has been following this lawyer fellow all day," he said. "He called me up tonight and told me that he was in Wapping. Poor guy!… I guess his wife will be sorry. We must find out where's she's living. What's the law about that, Colesberg – do I have to pay compensation when husband and wife are living apart?"

But Julius was absorbed in the tragedy.

"Have they found his body?" he asked in a hushed voice.

"No, but they're dragging the river, and they're sending a man up from Scotland Yard. If my advice had been followed we'd have called in Scotland Yard at first, and Atterman Brothers wouldn't have been short of the best floor detective in London."

"I didn't advise you to send for him,"

Mr Atterman looked at him reproachfully through his thick lenses.

"Boy," he said brokenly, "we're all in this. Don't go back on me now."

Detective-Inspector Finney, of Scotland Yard, knocked at the door of Mr Atterman's house at one o'clock in the morning. It appeared that the Thames Police had reported the occurrence to the Yard, and Mr Finney, who was on duty, had come personally to make inquiries.

He did not look like a detective; his face was neither thin nor ascetic, his eyes neither deep nor filled with a strange mystery; his hair was short, and he had cut himself while shaving. He was, moreover, in height some seventy-two inches and he was large-girthed.

He listened whilst Mr Atterman, with the assistance of Julius, described the circumstances which had led Peeker to his doom.

"Peeker? That's your floor man, isn't it?" asked Finney, without enthusiasm. "The fellow who's always writing to the Yard telling us where we're going wrong."

He did not seem to regret Peeker's untimely end with any great poignancy.

"I shouldn't think he's dead – those kind of people are never drowned," he said, and his ambiguity was offensive. "And who is Maber? Why do you think he's dead?"

The bag and the stained and crumpled clothes were produced from a cupboard. The officer inspected them dispassionately.

"This is undoubtedly blood," he said. "When did Mr Maber disappear?"

"He was last seen on Saturday night," said Julius. "I have that from a friend of mine who joined Mr Maber's party at the Trocadero but left rather early."

"And where does this Miss Storr work?"

They told him, speaking together.

"At Mabers – the place where the sale is?"

Julius and Mr Atterman nodded together.

"My wife tells me," said the detective, growing suddenly loquacious, "that there haven't been such bargains in London since she can remember. She bought three silk petticoats for the price of one. They tell me that Mabers have got Attermans skinned to death in the matter of prices."

"This," said Julius sternly, indicating his companion, "is Mr Atterman."

"Then," said the tactful police officer, "he'll be able to tell me whether that's true?"

"Quite untrue," said Mr Atterman hotly. "Mabers are underselling me because they're clearing out a lot of old stock at rubbish prices, and that's all its worth, and they're selling new stuff at cost. Maber is behaving most unscrupulously."

"That's the murdered man?" said the detective, fascinated.

"Well, no, it's the – the murderess, the girl we're telling you about. The girl who drowned Peeker."

"That's your floor detective?"

"Yes," said Mr Atterman impatiently. "She turned up on Sunday morning with a power of attorney, obviously wrung from the unwilling hands of her victim. Maber was murdered on Saturday night as soon as the document had been signed."

"And the commissioner of oaths – is he murdered too?" asked the detective. "I understand these things have to be signed before a commissioner."

That rather staggered him.

"I don't know the details of the crimes; you'll probably get them best from Miss Storr."

"Very good, gentlemen." The detective took up the bag and examined it. "Who cut this open?"

"I cut it open in the interests of justice," said Mr Atterman virtuously.

"Where did you get the bag?"

How the man rattled on! Atterman grew quite exasperated. He never even mentioned the drowned Peeker.

"It was taken from the safe in Maber's office by Mr Julius Colesberg – this gentleman" – he did a little introducing – "the junior partner."

"I had better take that down," said the detective, and lugged out his notebook again.

"Make that 'late junior partner,'" said Julius nervously. "I don't want to sail under false colours."

"But you were junior partner when this bag was taken from the safe?" said the detective.

He was one of those stupid men who preferred to fasten himself on the visible felony; to him a larceny in the hand was worth a hundred murders in the bush.

"No, I wasn't exactly senior – junior – in the firm, when I took the bag. As a matter of fact" – Julius became more and more incoherent – "I took the bag because I promised my friend Maber that I would take it. You see?"

"No, I don't see," said the obtuse officer of the law. "Did Mr Maber tell you that his bloodstained shirt would be in that bag?"

"No, he didn't," admitted Julius.

"Has the bag ever been kept in the safe?"

"No, that's it," said Atterman eagerly. "The girl put the bag in the safe." He stepped back to observe the effect of his portentous words. The detective did not so much as say "Ah ha!"

"What I want to know is this," he said with exemplary patience. "Mr Maber told you to take the bag from the safe?"

"Yes and no," said Julius. It seemed an artful kind of answer to him.

"Did you know the bag was there?"

"Yes."

"Did you know Miss Storr put it there?"

"I did."

"And did you take the bag from the safe, knowing Miss Storr had put it there?"

"That is the fact," said Julius, who thought that this sensible man had at last taken a plain, common-sense view of a complicated situation.

"Very good," said the detective. "Now, when did you take it?"

Julius looked at Atterman and Atterman looked at the clock.

"It must have been about two o'clock yesterday morning."

116

"In the night?"

"The morning," said Julius. It sounded better that way.

"How did you get in?"

"Through the staff door."

The inspector jotted this down too.

"With a key?"

Julius nodded.

"A pass-key, I suppose?"

Julius nodded again.

"Which was given to you as managing director?"

"You've got it in one, my dear fellow," said Julius.

"Were you a director when you used that pass-key and opened that safe and took that bag?"

"No, I wasn't," admitted Julius. "But for goodness' sake keep to the subject of the murder."

"I'll get back to the murder in a minute. The point is this, gentlemen: we've had a complaint at the Yard that a patrolman in this division saw a man breaking out of Mabers some time after two o'clock yesterday morning, that he pursued him and eventually lost sight of him. Now I've heard how you got in – how did you get out?"

"Through a window," said Julius, growing desperate as the prison gates opened inch by inch for him. "I want to tell you about Mr Maber. He was a very kind, good-hearted man, but rather influenced by women. This girl – "

"Never mind about this girl." The inspector was almost offensive. "Did you jump out of that window or didn't you?"

"I've told you I did."

"And you were chased by the police?"

"Of course I was."

"Then come along with me," said the inspector, almost unexpectedly.

In a dim, impersonal way Julius realised that somebody called Julius Colesberg was walking side by side down a dismal street towards a building which advertised its character by the display of a large blue lamp. This Julius was made to stand near a steel pen, the other Julius watching curiously, and was told that he would be detained on suspicion of having broken and entered the premises of Maber & Maber between the hours of 2 and 4 a.m., and further with assaulting Police-Constable Thomas Wellbeloved in the execution of his duty.

"Wellbeloved?" croaked Julius in his dream. "What an extraordinary name!"

Mr Atterman, very short of breath, had loyally accompanied Julius to the station. Now, plucking up his courage, he spoke his mind.

"What about the murders?" he asked in a deep, booming voice that did not seem to belong to him.

"We'll go and see about those murders now," said the inspector. "Perhaps you'd like to come along?"

"No, no, thank you very much," said Mr Atterman hastily. "You know where to find me – I'm Atterman of Atterman Brothers."

"I know who you are," said the inspector, and there was so much of menace in his tone that Mr Atterman suddenly went cold.

10

No word of the Wapping Stairs murder appeared in the morning newspaper that Barbara scanned at seven o'clock as she sipped her coffee. Nor had her night's rest been disturbed by the call of policemen or other representatives of the law. Probably, had a charge been preferred against Julius Colesberg, she would have been called upon in her capacity of prosecutrix, but no such charge was made. He was sent home, more dead than alive, at half-past three o'clock, with the warning that he might at any moment be rearrested and charged with felony, housebreaking, conversion of property, receiving the same knowing it to be stolen, conspiracy to defraud, illegal possession, and assaulting the police. Each station official who interviewed him gave him a different version of his offence, except that they were all unanimous as to the charge of assault. His experience and these horrific warnings were not conducive to sleep. Haggard-eyed, he sat up the remainder of the night in Mr Atterman's study and got what comfort he could from the magnate's assurance that Barbara Storr's hours of liberty were few.

"I hand it to these London policemen," said Mr Atterman enthusiastically. "They've got a quiet, silly way with 'em that kind of gives you a wrong impression, but when they get their noses down to the bloodstained trail of crime they never let up till they have the thug behind bars."

Julius shivered.

"You've got to get me out of this trouble," he said pettishly. "You know perfectly well that I didn't want to burgle that wretched bag!

You and your fearful Live Wire between you have got me to the prison gates."

"Listen, boy," said Mr Atterman, dropping his hand affectionately on his friend's shoulder. "When you come out there's a position for you in my store. I'm not the sort of bird that forgets anybody who's been useful to me. Maudie was only saying last night – "

"Who's Maudie?" grumbled Julius.

A slow, sweet smile illuminated the dark, unpleasant features of Mr Atterman.

"She's wonderful!" he breathed. "If it wasn't for this Maber business I'd be the happiest man in the world tonight. She's going right back into the orchestra tomorrow, and the peroxide blond who is leading can either take the euphonium and a back seat or quit. That baby wouldn't stay another minute at Mabers when she knew her Atty wanted her."

Julius was gazing at him open-eyed. He had never seen Mr Atterman in his tender moments. It was an unforgettable sight.

They, too, searched the papers for news of the tragedy; but whilst they were disappointed, Barbara was ignorant of what she was missing.

Maudie's letter puzzled her a little. The reference to the underlined past was bewildering. She had had no "past" in common with Maudie, any more than she had with Mr Lark.

From information received, Maudie had not put in an appearance at the band, but her return had been actually billed, and spies going across to Attermans had returned with stories of an ornamental announcement of the return of Maudina, the silver cornetist from the leading opera houses of Europe. Moreover, the soon-to-be-deposed orchestra leader had been half a note flat all the previous afternoon.

It was ten o'clock and she had opened all her letters and dictated most of the replies, when Mr Lark flew into her room in a state of agitation, a cheque in his hand.

"What's this, Miss Storr?" he asked. His voice held its old querulous ring. Contact with money brought out all that was worst in his nature. "Who is Hammett?"

She took the cheque from his hand, examined the amount and the signature, and almost collapsed.

"Hammett is a lawyer," she said faintly, and Mr Lark was momentarily relieved. It seemed right that lawyers should receive large cheques. If it had been for ten thousand Mr Lark would have been unperturbed.

"That's OK," he said. "Only I had never seen the name before, and I was scared – but, of course, a lawyer – "

She shook her head, incapable of immediate explanation.

"It's – it's a forgery," she managed to say at last. "I didn't draw the cheque at all. And it doesn't belong to our series, anyway."

Mr Lark stared horror-stricken at the oblong slip.

"I noticed that. I said to my young lady... Shall I phone to the bank – "

She stopped him.

"Not yet. Just give me a few minutes to think it over, Mr Lark. This is rather a serious matter for me."

She meant really that it was rather a serious matter for the absent Mr Maber. If she took action, exposure would be inevitable; if she did not take action, she was condoning a felony. At that critical moment of her affairs Alan Stewart called with three half-page spaces up one sleeve and innumerable treble columns up the other.

"And you're the luckiest girl – " he began, and saw her troubled face. "What on earth is the matter?" he asked, all the business man in him disappearing at the sight of her distress.

She must tell him something – he ought to know. Without stopping to analyse his right to information, she felt that an advertising man who didn't know was something of an anomaly. He was rather like a clock without works.

"A man has forged a cheque," she said miserably.

"Well, prosecute him. Do you know who it is?"

She nodded.

"I can't prosecute him, because, if I do, he'll – he'll tell something I don't wish to be known."

Alan's face went suddenly bleak.

121

"Somebody – is blackmailing you?" he said unsteadily.

"Yes," said Barbara, avoiding his eyes.

"I'm sorry." He sat down opposite her, and, reaching out his hand, grasped hers, and she was too unhappy to offer any objection to his action. "Who is it?" he asked gently.

"Hammett. You won't know him; he's a little lawyer – "

"I know all about Hammett," he interrupted. "Everybody in London knows Hammett. He's the thieves' last refuge."

He might have added "and the blackmailer's stay," but did not wish to hurt her.

"Can't you tell *me*?" he asked gently.

She shook her head.

"Is it" – he found it hard to say – "a man?"

She was staring out of the window, her face averted. Her lips moved.

She was staring out of the window, her face averted. Her lips moved.

"Yes," he saw rather than heard.

Alan's hand tightened momentarily.

"Somebody you're rather – fond of?" His voice was hoarse and unnatural. She found time to wonder if he had given up wearing woollies too early in the year. The weather was so treacherous.

She looked at him quickly.

"Do you know?" she asked.

"I can guess," he said bitterly. "You're trying to protect him, and Hammett, knowing your – association, has forged the cheque, expecting that you will not prosecute."

"What am I to do?" She was looking out of the window again. "If I have him arrested…the whole thing will come out, and that would mean absolute – well, it would be terrible!"

He wondered what Mr Maber, with his old-fashioned distaste for scandal and his horror of publicity, would say to this, what advice he would give in the situation. Barbara's position was a very responsible one. She not only held her own but her employer's honour in her hand.

"Mr Maber doesn't know, of course – about this?"

"No," said Barbara, "and I don't want him to know. He trusts me absolutely. I must find some way of saving his name."

So it was as bad as that! Alan grew cold. He even sneezed. It was an absurd interpolation, verging on the grotesque. She looked at him anxiously. These men who had been in the trenches were very careless about their underwear. Perhaps he had a landlady who drank and forgot to air his shirts. Women like that should be punished by law.

"It might help if you told me a little more," he was saying. "I don't want to hurt you or ask you to take me too much into your confidence – I can guess a whole lot. Hammett could not blackmail you unless the thing he knew about your – about your friend was unusually terrible. I quite understand your wanting to protect him; being what you are, you would not let a man down, not – not if you were fond of him." His voice grew husky.

"I am fond of him," she nodded simply. "You see, I've known him ever since I was a little girl. I remember the first time I ever saw him. He came to my aunt's house to tea. It was Christmas Eve and the mistletoe was up over the door, and he – he kissed me."

Her voice broke. The head of the unknown would have also broken if it had been within reach of Alan Stewart's clenched fist.

There was one question he wanted to ask badly, but could not bring himself to learn the dreaded truth.

"You're not married to him?" He blurted the words, and did not dare face her when she turned.

"Married? How ridiculous! No, of course not!"

Alan Stewart sighed heavily.

Of course not! Those kind of men never married. Or else they were married at an early age and had to live apart from their wives because they drank or were violent.

"I'm fond of him and he's fond of me, but there was never any question…oh, how stupid the idea seems! I never dreamed you would think that I should marry that kind of man, lovable as he is."

He felt he had a duty to his kind.

123

"You might reform him," he suggested loyally. "Those are the kind of men who sometimes respond to matrimony."

"He doesn't need reforming," she said with spirit. "He's the best, dearest, kindest, sweetest man alive!"

Evidently she liked him. It was foolish to attempt to shake her faith in one who was probably a heartless scoundrel.

"I don't know what steps to take about Mr Hammett," she said. "Not that I shall be able to do very much, because he will have gone by now. He had a ticket for Canada, according to his wife's statement, and I suppose that by this time he's on the high seas. They can't be too high for my liking – I hope he is very sick!"

She roused herself and smiled at him. But at the same time he had a feeling that she was looking a little anxiously for his approval.

"Perhaps that is best," he said. It was a formal thing to say, but for the life of him he could not enthuse. "The only thing is, unless you inform the bank today you will not be able to recover your money. I think on the whole, if I were you, I should do as you've done."

He took some papers out of his pocket.

"Do you mind going over the question of these spaces?" he asked politely.

She was a little disappointed in him. That he could switch so quickly from her great trouble, knowing, as she guessed, all the circumstances, and, brushing aside her troubles and difficulties, plunge into the question of mundane advertisements, was unpardonable. They parted somewhat stiffly. Alan was sore, and smarted from the hurt that comes to every man's vanity when he discovers that the girl of his heart had chosen elsewhere for her partner. She was annoyed at the mercenary aspect of him, and a little anxious about his huskiness. Probably he smoked too much.

He was nearing his own office when he remembered that he had a piece of information for her, which in the stress of the moment he had forgotten to give. On the previous day she asked him to make some inquiries about Maud Deane, more especially in relation to her father; for Barbara was curious to know in what way the continued presence of the girl in Mabers jeopardised her parent's pension. He brighted up at this excuse for telephoning her.

"Yes?" Her voice was prim and uncompromising.

"Oh, Barbara, I've just remembered that you asked me to find out about Maudie Deane."

"Yes?" Her natural curiosity got the better of her dignity. "Did you find out?"

"Yes. Her father is one of the chief warders at Pentonville Prison. If you remember, that fact came out when the breach of promise case was heard."

There was no answer from the other end of the phone.

"Did you hear me, Barbara?"

"Yes, I heard you – Mr Stewart." Her voice sounded so sharp that it chilled him.

"That was all I wanted to say. Good-bye." He banged down the receiver savagely, in the say that young men have when their telephonic conversations with beautiful ladies are of an unsatisfactory nature.

Barbara sat back in her chair, her hand to her head. Maudie knew! Of course, that was Mr Deane's job. She remembered now that Maudie had once told her how her father could entertain her by the hour with his stories of prisons and prisoners. Maudie knew! The garrulous old man must have discovered Maber amongst his charges, and this was the result.

Again she read the letter from the soloist. Maudie would not speak, and, if she did not speak, no great harm would result. But Atterman was her sweetheart, and what more natural than that she should confide into his ecstatic ears the story of William Maber's downfall? Then, indeed, the mischief would be done. Maber's secret, a secret no longer, would be blazoned in red letters on the front of Atterman's store. She pictured huge banners, decorated with the prison totem, aimed derisively at Atterman's old rival. What could she do?

It was Police-Constable Albuera who pointed the way to a solution.

"Will you see Mr Finney?" he asked in a hushed voice. He gave her the impression that she was about to be honoured. That she might not overlook this fact he added: "He's an inspector from the Yard."

It was about the cheque – the bank had discovered it! Or perhaps Hammett had been arrested! She nodded.

"Good morning, miss." Mr Finney was very stout and cheery and beamed delightfully. "I saw Mr Atterman last night – " he began.

Barbara listened in silence, and at the end:

"I suppose there's a perfectly simple explanation for the clothes and shirt," he stated rather than enquired.

Barbara nodded.

"A natural but unfortunate one," she said, with the ghost of a smile in her eyes. "Mr Maber got into very serious trouble on Boat Race night – with the – er – police, I believe. There was even some talk of his having bitten the ear of a commissionaire, but that I will never believe."

The genial inspector opened his mouth wide.

"He's doing time?" he gurgled.

"A month," said Barbara shortly, and the music of laughter came out to Albuera Sturman, and he speculated upon which one his superior had told her, for Inspector Finney was a notable raconteur.

When the inspector had dried his eyes and restrained himself from a further outburst, he told her of the detention of Julius, and the girl was troubled.

"As a matter of fact, he had a right to be on the premises," she said. "Although I've accepted the dissolution of partnership on behalf of Mr Maber, I practically gave him permission to come back. You can't proceed with that charge, inspector."

"I can't proceed with that, but I've got to proceed with the assault," said the inspector, equally serious. "He gave the constable a whack on the jaw, and you can't get over that, not if you tried from now to Christmas."

Very wisely, Barbara did not attempt to get over that.

"What will happen to him?"

The inspector shrugged his shoulders.

"A month or six weeks," he said carelessly.

"In Pentonville?" gasped Barbara.

The officer looked up to the ceiling in thought.

"Yes, in Pentonville," he agreed.

"Then he must not be charged," said Barbara vigorously. "Under no circumstances could I allow Mr Colesberg to go to Pentonville. Haven't you any other prison you could put him into?"

Again the officer considered.

"There's Wandsworth," he suggested. He was rather like an estate agent offering a desirable alternative. "But I think he would go to Pentonville."

He explained that in cases of crimes committed north of the Thames the delinquents were sent to Pentonville; south of the Thames, to Wandsworth.

"Then he'd go to Pentonville," said Barbara, "and that mustn't happen. I want you to do your best for me, Mr Finney. The unfortunate officer must of course be compensated for his injury. I will see to that."

The officer demurred. Barbara, in her sweetest mood, pleaded.

"Don't you see, Mr Finney, I've taken all this trouble to keep Mr Maber's secret, and if Julius Colesberg goes to prison they're sure to meet."

"That's true," said the officer thoughtfully. "Prisoners *do* see one another in Pentonville, although its a large place. Unless, of course, one of the gentlemen in question is going to be hanged, and I'm afraid that won't happen to Mr Colesberg. I'll see what I can do."

He rose and shook hands.

"I wouldn't say anything to Mr Atterman about this," he said beamingly. "There's another little matter which is just a wee bit more serious which we're investigating at the moment. It ought to be cleared up today or tomorrow, and then I think he can know."

He did not explain any further, and Barbara was not interested.

Whatever relief this exchange of confidences gave her was short-lived. At half-past two came a moment of terrible crisis. It began with a phone message from the bank.

"Can I see you?" asked the manager urgently.

"Come along," invited Barbara, and put down the telephone with an uneasy feeling. She hated banks; they represented to her the tyranny of commercial life. Not for nothing did they occupy all the best corner lots. Now she had an unhappy feeling that the forgery had been discovered.

The bank manager was a briefly spoken man, and had little outside interests but the weather. When he had stated definitely that it was a fine day he came to the point.

"You're overrunning the constable, young lady," he said. "I've just had Colesberg's cheque for seven thousand presented. I've paid out very big accounts, and the position is that at the moment you are three thousand overdrawn."

Barbara's heart almost stopped beating.

"What can I do?" she asked.

"You'd better draw on Mr Maber's private account," he said. "He doesn't bank with us; in fact, I don't know where he banks. It is very unlikely, in any case, that he would carry large balances. Can't you borrow ten thousand?"

"Couldn't I mortgage the business?" she answered daringly.

The bank manager shook his head.

"Not without all the world knowing about it," he said. "Your best course is to see somebody who has a floating balance – somebody like Atterman."

"Atterman?" she said, aghast. "He wouldn't lend me the money."

The bank manager smiled knowingly.

"Ask him," he suggested.

Without hesitation, Barbara put on her hat and went across to Attermans.

The first person she saw in the store was Mr Minkey, who scowled at her terrifically. The Live Wire was under a cloud. No longer did Mr Atterman introduce him to strangers with a proud, possessive wave of hand, as a farmer introduces his prize Shorthorn. The great man passed him in the store with no more than a curt nod. Even the lower grades of employee were inclined to neglect him as though he were an ordinary man. Minkey felt his position keenly; never saw the window in which he had slept so peacefully, unconscious of the sensation he had created, without seeing also several shades of red.

"Good afternoon, Mr Minkey." Barbara was sweetness itself. "Do you know where I can find Mr Atterman?"

The Live Wire jerked his thumb to the elevator, not trusting himself to speak.

A messenger took in her name, and she heard Mr Atterman's voice through the half-opened door.

"Tell her to come in."

He was standing behind his table, a triumphant smirk on his face. Maudie was the other occupant of the room; she nodded distantly.

"Well, young lady, you've come in time to see my little show!"

He waved his hand to the wall behind her, and, turning, she saw a large white bill printed in red, the paint still wet.

MABER IS IN JAIL!
HENCE THE SALE
ATTERMANS FOR
HONEST DEALING.

Somehow Barbara felt that she was not likely to borrow money from this law-abiding man.

11

Then the secret was out! Maber's misfortune would soon be common property.

She looked at Maudie; the girl averted her eyes.

"Very pretty," said Barbara steadily, "but you're not going to exhibit that before your establishment?"

"That's just what is going up, miss, in an hour's time."

Barbara shook her head.

"I don't think so," she said quietly. "In the first place, it will cost you more money in libel damages than you would care to pay."

"He's in jail, isn't he?" he demanded.

"He was dead the last time I heard of him," she said. "Murdered by a designing woman. I rather fancy you found his bloodstained relics – they were stolen by Mr Colesberg, who will be arrested ten minutes after that poster goes up. So far I've kept him clear, not because I like him, but because I couldn't very well take him to court without exposing the whole affair."

She looked at him speculatively.

"I rather fancy that you also will be in jail for receiving. Inspector Finney and I are having a conference on the subject."

"There's no libel in the truth," he said uncomfortably.

"There's libel in suggesting he's dishonest. All Mr Maber did was bite a policeman's ear – there's nothing dishonest about that," said Barbara. "Obviously he didn't like the policeman. It was an honest expression of his feelings."

Atterman looked at the poster and felt less confident.

"Besides, there's a law – even my private policeman knows this," Barbara went on – "if warders carry stories out of prison they're liable to lose their pensions."

Maudie bridled.

"If you suggest, Miss Storr, that I've told any stories to Mr Atterman, you're very much mistaken and have got the wrong end of the stick. And if you try to frighten me, miss – "

"The point is, Mr Atterman" – Barbara had really no time to bother with Maudie Deane – "I came to see you about borrowing some money. I'm overdrawn at the bank, and my manager suggested that I should come to you."

Atterman gaped at her in astonishment.

"Come to me?" he said, amazed. "Do you imagine for one moment I will lend you...how much do you want?"

"Ten thousand," said Barbara.

Mr Atterman's flabbergasted silence was Maudie's opportunity.

"My pa certainly did see Mr Maber. I'm not going to say he didn't. He saw him the day he came in – "

Barbara waved her to silence.

"I had come intending to do a deal with you," she began and Mr Atterman laughed sardonically. "But it is impossible to have any business dealings in view of that." She pointed to the placard. "It would be a disgraceful thing in any circumstances to make an attack upon the personal character of a business competitor. In this case it is not only disgraceful, but foolish."

"That bill is going out," said Mr Atterman emphatically.

Barbara snapped her fingers.

"Then you'll go out – like that," she said, and stalked from the room.

She went back to her office a very depressed girl, and found Lark waiting at the top of the stairs to intercept her.

"Do you know Mr Elbury?" he asked. "Marcus Elbury – a great friend of the governor's? I've often heard him speak about him."

She shook her head.

"Why?" she asked.

131

"He's there." He pointed along the passage. "Waiting for you. I had him shown into the office."

She hurried along, wondering whether this mysterious Mr Elbury might offer any help to her in her time of trouble.

He was a tall, broad-shouldered, good-looking man, and if he was not an American he had been in America long enough to have acquired American habits. She was surprised to learn that he was English-born, if American by nationality.

"I've just arrived from Paris." He shook hands with her heartily. "Too bad you've had all this trouble, Miss Storr," he said.

He was uneasy about something, kept glancing nervously around.

"I heard about this sale of yours, and wondered if you might be in some sort of difficulty."

"I'm in a very great difficulty," she smiled ruefully. "I've played ducks and drakes with Mr Maber's bank balance, and I'm overdrawn."

He seemed relieved to hear this.

"Is that all," he said. And then, to her delight, he took out a cheque-book from his pocket. "How much do you want?"

"Immediately, three thousand. I may want ten. My bank manager advises ten."

"And he's wise," said Mr Elbury, and filled up a cheque for that amount under her astonished eyes.

"Have you – have you heard from Mr Maber?"

He nodded.

"Yes, I've heard," he said, and something in his tone told her that he was anxious to avoid being questioned further. "When the heart's young," he said oracularly, "men do queer things. You're sure this is enough?" He seemed anxious to increase the amount.

"Oh, it's quite enough, thank you, Mr Elbury," she said gratefully. "And if you get into touch with Mr Maber, will you tell him everything is going splendidly? Especially his money. I don't know what he'll think of me," she said with an uncomfortable laugh.

"He thinks the world of you, little girl," said Mr Elbury solemnly. "He thinks you're just he cutest – well, he thinks a whole lot of you. As I was saying, when the heart is young a man does things in the heat of the moment, or from a sense of honour, that he wouldn't have done if I'd been there."

"You were not at the Empire?"

"Oh, yes, I was." Mr Elbury was full of surprises. "You mean when they pinched him? Sure I was! I thought they'd let him go, and I didn't know he'd been arrested until I called at the court to make certain and found he'd been sent down. As I said to your Secretary of State – how do you call him? – Home Secretary – it was a mistake that might naturally occur. It was Big Bill Langstead, an old friend of mine from Cincinnati, that did the biting. Bill was always partial to a rough house."

"Then it wasn't Mr Maber? I'm so glad!" she said.

"No, I guess it wasn't Mr Maber," said Elbury carefully. "As I told the Secretary of State, that man did nothing but sit down and admire the view. He did get into a rough house eventually by trying to help Bill, and I guess that was why the coppers took him."

"Then he's imprisoned innocently?" gasped Barbara.

Mr Elbury scratched his chin.

"Yes, he was," he admitted, and glanced that uneasy glance of his towards the door.

It was not Police-Constable Albuera Sturman who caused the apprehension so visible on his jolly face. At him he grinned.

"I won't stay, Miss Storr," he said. "The only thing I'd like to tell you is this: that when the heart is young – "

"You've told me that before," she smiled.

"I guess I did," admitted the American unhappily. "But I want to tell you this: that Mr Maber thoroughly approves of this sale. He thoroughly approves of your firing that dud partner. He's going to give you a big interest in the business, and he wants you to think twice before you sell."

A great load rolled from her mind.

"Does he really?" she asked eagerly. "How lovely of him! Have you seen him in prison?"

"As to this man Atterman," said Mr Elbury earnestly, "I want you to believe that he's no American. I shouldn't like anybody to think ill of America. His sister is American by marriage…" He paused here and looked at her anxiously as though he expected her to say something. When she refrained, he hurried on: "Atterman's just a slick little fellow that's made good by accident. Mr Maber says that when he comes back, in about six months' time – "

She gave a gasp of dismay.

"In six months' time? He only got a month," she said.

Mr Elbury nodded very gently.

"That's true," he said; "he got a month. He's going home to America with me, and he wants me to say" – this was the thing he'd been trying to say all along, and now he spoke with an obvious effort – "that – you're – to – give – her – anything – in – reason!"

Barbara looked at him open-eyed.

"Give whom?"

Mr Elbury was embarrassed.

"When the heart is young – " he began.

"Yes, yes, I know all about that." She was not even amused. "But to whom am I to give anything she wants?"

"The whole thing is very unfortunate – *very* unfortunate," said Marcus Elbury, twisting his hat round and round by the brim, like a schoolboy who had been caught in an unlawful act. "The information we had was, after this terrible affair – "

"Which terrible affair?" she persisted.

He looked at her pathetically – like a wounded steer.

"Mighty good of you, Miss Storr," he said slowly. "I appreciate it, and I'm sure Mr Maber will appreciate it – I mean your going on as though you didn't know anything about it. My address is the Hotel Majestic, Paris. I'm flying back by airplane this evening. My bank is the Guaranty Paris Branch, and I've given orders so that you can draw on me for any amount you want. 'Tippitty, New York,' will always find me."

Abruptly he reached out and gripped her hand.

"We shall never forget you – either of us," he said, and before she realised it he was gone, leaving her more mystified than ever.

Her first act was to call up the bank and tell the manager that the cheque was on its way. Her next was to call Alan Stewart, and he was cold and formal.

"Come round at once," she ordered, and the taxi did not go fast enough for Mr Stewart.

In a few words she told him, and as she unfolded the story of Mr Maber's lapse from grace she saw a queer look come to his face.

"In prison?" he whispered.

"Unjustly," said Barbara. "Of course, I knew he hadn't bitten anybody. He had awfully tender teeth and could never eat anything unless it was boiled."

"But I thought – you were talking about a man," he blurted. "I mean somebody you were…fond of…who used to kiss you. I mean – under the mistletoe, when you were very small…"

He tried desperately to escape from the tangle into which he had drifted. Barbara froze suddenly.

"I see. You thought I was confessing the story of my humid past. Thank you!"

"Of course, I never believed for one moment – "

"Thank you," said Barbara crushingly. "I don't think we need discuss that matter any further. The only point is: what did Elbury mean by 'giving her all she wanted'? He can't refer to Mrs Hammett, because he doesn't know of her existence. And it can't possible be Maudie, unless – "

She knit her brows in thought, going mentally over the features and demeanour of all the goddesses of the silks and lingerie. But Mr Maber was not that kind. She sighed. The whole thing was inexplicable.

"The point I wanted to see you about, Mr Stewart, was this terrible poster which Attermans are going to put out."

The two upper windows in Attermans' facia were open. Men were lowering long ropes, and soon the poster itself would appear on the ground level and be hoisted into position. But before that happened something occurred to make Mr Atterman change his mind. She saw the ropes going up and the windows closed. Evidently the threat of the libel had had its effect. In truth, Mr Atterman was so far gone in rage, so exalted by his discovery, that neither threat of libel nor personal violence would have stopped him. The reason had been something quite different. One of his mommas – the real one – had called him up to ask him to dinner, and in his high spirits he had done what he very seldom did – he had talked business, and told her the story of his rival's humiliation.

"You do dot, and I come and clomp your 'ead!" said his momma. "Do you want your sister Rachel to go to jail, you poor simp?"

Mr Atterman went to Hampstead to call upon his momma, with the horrible feeling that he was not quite right in his head.

12

Long after the store was closed Barbara sat in her office, puzzling over this queer but providential visit of Marcus Elbury. She strolled down into the shop; assistants were covering the dresses in long holland sheets; the day cleaners were sweeping the floor, and there was a stream of hurrying girls moving to the staff door. She stood watching them, bidding them a mechanical good night, and then, when there was a gap, drifted down the stone stairs to the timekeeper's office. She wanted to see the night watchman because, in the excitement of the day, no takings had been banked and the safe held a much larger sum of money than she cared to think about.

He had just come on duty, and in a few words she explained to him the necessity for wakefulness.

"If you must sleep, would you mind sleeping with your back against the safe?" she begged.

"I never sleep at night, miss," protested the night watchman. "I admit that I dozed off the other night, but it's my belief that I was drugged. I remember my tea coming – "

"Well, if you're drugged tonight," she smiled, "will you summon up enough strength to crawl to the safe and tie yourself to the handle?"

The timekeeper was struggling into his coat. He was, if anything, an older servant of the firm than the night watchman; a grim and taciturn man, who never spoke except to say, "You're late, miss."

She walked over to him and, for the second time since she had been with Mr Maber, spoke to him.

"We've kept you rather late this week, Mr Beale," she said.

"Yes, miss."

"I hope you will mark up your overtime. You were here till midnight one night."

"Yes, miss," he said again.

"Monday?" she suggested.

"And Tuesday," he said. He had a sour way of speaking, but she thought that was due to lack of practice in the art of talking at all. "Wednesday morning I was so tired that I could hardly keep my eyes open. I told Mr Maber – "

"Not Mr Maber," she said gently. Evidently he was still tired. "You mean Mr Lark?"

"Mr Maber," insisted the man, "when he came in here about twelve o'clock in the morning, just before lunch. I said to Mr Maber – "

"But you're mistaken, Beale. Mr Maber hasn't been here this week."

His bushy eyebrows rose. He hated being contradicted by a girl whose mother wasn't born when he joined Mabers.

"He was here on Wednesday," he said deliberately. "Him and that other gentleman. And I said to him – "

She was gazing at him in amazement.

"But surely you're mistaken? Mr Maber hasn't been here?"

"Yes, he has, miss," was the astounding reply. "He was here on Wednesday morning. I put him in the book."

He turned back to his box, unlocked a cupboard, took out a thin ledger and turned the pages.

"There you are, miss – '11.55, Mr Maber, with gentleman,'" he read.

She stared at him, aghast.

"Did he come into the building?"

"No, miss. He just come in and said, 'Good morning, Beale,' and I told him that Mrs Maber had just gone upstairs – "

"Do you mind letting me sit down in your chair?" said Barbara faintly. "You told him Mrs Maber had gone upstairs? And then – ?"

"And then he went out again, him and the other gentleman, and I said to him, though I don't think he was listening, that what with late nights at my time of life – "

She wasn't listening either. Mr Maber had come, and Beale had told him that Mrs Maber had just gone upstairs, and then he'd gone out again! But Mr Maber was in prison; it was impossible that he could have been on the premises on Wednesday.

"How was he dressed?"

"In a brown suit, miss, with a black and white spotted tie. I thought it was a bit gay for an old gentleman – !"

The suit she had taken to him; she particularly remembered the tie. Then where was he? How had he got out? In what manner had he made his escape from prison?

"How did you know Mrs Maber had come in?"

"He told me her name, miss – a flash-looking lady."

"That was Mrs Maber," said Barbara; "or rather, the woman who called herself Mrs Maber."

"I never make any inquiries into people's private lives," said Beale virtuously. "If anybody calls herself 'Mrs Maber,' she's Mrs Maber to me."

Barbara dithered upstairs to sort out, amidst the confusion of her impressions, some logical explanation. She wondered, if she went up to Pentonville Prison and knocked on the door and asked if Mr Maber was in, whether it would be likely that a satisfactory answer would be afforded her. And yet they must know. Almost for a second she decided on that action, but then the absurdity of it brought her to laughter and to the edge of hysteria. She wished Alan would come, and, as though influenced by her thoughts, the night watchman arrived to announce that that young man was waiting at what he facetiously described as "the stage door," and she grabbed her hat and coat and went down hastily to meet him.

They turned out of Lawton Street into Marlborough Avenue, and as they did so a car dashed up to the front of Mabers, the door was flung open, and Mr Atterman sprang down. He was wearing no hat, was obviously in great and frantic haste. At the sight of the girl he ran towards her with a cry which was scarcely human.

"Miss Storr," he said agitatedly, "can I have a word with you?"

"I don't want to go back to my office. Can't you tell me here?"

He looked at Alan, and Mr Stewart very discreetly withdrew.

"You want a cheque for ten thousand," said Mr Atterman rapidly. "I can let you have it – I'll give it to you right now."

"I don't want it at all, thank you," she said, astonished at this unexpected offer from the enemy. "I've had the money from Mr Maber."

"You're not mad at me? Anything I've said to you that's offensive, believe me, Miss Storr, I'm deeply sorry for. You're a lady in ten thousand – in twenty thousand," he added extravagantly. "I'm sure Mr Maber ought to be a very proud man to have a young lady like you around him. And as to his being in prison, why, anybody – "

"He's not in prison. It was quite a mistake. The Home Office released him."

That solution came to her at that moment, and she remembered Marcus Elbury's words.

"I'm glad; it was disgraceful to arrest a gen'leman like that. You see, Miss Storr, Maber's an old friend of our family's."

Here was extraordinary news.

"He knew my sister." Mr Atterman went on, speaking very fast as though he wanted to get the worst over. "She's in America now, married and doing very well. I never knew about it till my mother told me tonight," he said with great truth, "but Rachel and Mr Maber were mighty good friends – at least, they met. In fact, Mr Maber got my sister out of very bad trouble; that's queer, isn't it? Got her out of a bad scrape, and at the Empire, too – committed perjury to save her."

"Indeed?" said Barbara. She was pinching herself and knew that she was awake.

"There was no excuse for her – none whatever. But she was always an impulsive girl…when the heart is young…"

He was becoming rapidly incoherent. Barbara listened, and heard the story of Mr Maber's first escapade. It was the story of a great rag at the Empire many years before; of a night that had ended disastrously; of a lady who in the excitement of the moment had endeavoured to rescue him from the hands of the police, and had found herself marched to Marlborough Street; of a chivalrous man who, finding he had compromised the lady, had offered her marriage by special licence, an offer which had been accepted...

"Rachel shouldn't have married him, but she was always a tender-hearted girl and didn't like hurting people's feelings. Momma always said that it was the unkindest thing she'd ever done to Willie – that was her husband."

"Was she married?" gasped Barbara.

"Yes, she was married. That was what made it so extremely awkward...they parted at the church door, Mr Maber and she. It was very awkward, because she had never told him anything about Willie, and went off to Boston by the next boat. In fact, she asked him not to say a word about it. Only Momma knew. Rachel was very thoughtless, but when the heart is young..."

The patient Alan Stewart showed this quality in an unusual degree. He waited and waited, and was still waiting for nearly half an hour, pacing up and down before the dark windows of the store.

"Of course, I told momma that under the circumstances it was stupid to oppose the union of Maudie and me. We're to be married next week," said Mr Atterman. "And, Miss Storr, I'd like to talk to you about this business which Mr Maber wants to sell. If it hadn't been for that bonehead Colesberg I'd have made a reasonable offer... You'll think it over, won't you, Miss Storr?" he pleaded.

Barbara promised, and ran to the waiting Alan and grabbed him by the arm.

"I'm not going home," she said. "You are taking me to the Ritz-Carlton grill, and I want a big dinner and a small bottle of champagne. But first I must send a wire."

The cab stopped at Regent Street and, releasing herself gently, Barbara got down. She tore off a foreign telegraph blank and sent a wire addressed:

To Marcus Elbury, Hotel Majestic, Paris. Tell him that Rachel was married all the time. – Barbara.

The morning brought Inspector Finney, with news. Mr Hammett, the solicitor, had been arrested off Gravesend; and incidentally Peeker, the sleuth, who, seeing as he thought his quarry escape him, had daringly plunged into the water and, gripping the back of a ship's dinghy, had allowed himself to be rowed to the side of the *Silina* on his errand of detection, was released from what promised to be a very uncomfortable voyage. The money in Hammett's pocket was almost intact.

"You know Mr Maber was released, I suppose?"

"I guessed so," she said.

"Yes, he was released on the second day. The police had made a mistake in identification, and as soon as they found their error the Home Office was notified and he was let out on a fine. What surprises me is that he didn't come round to see you. You'll have to charge this bird, I'm afraid. He's confessed the forgery – he thought that was why I wanted him. As a matter of fact, we were after the skipper, and if Hammett hadn't been talkative he'd have got away with it."

Mr Maber returned that very afternoon by the three-thirty train – a bronzed, jaunty Mr Maber who almost pranced to his room. He made no reference either to her telegram or the letter she had sent to Dover to meet him when she heard of his intended return. The weight of years had fallen from his shoulders; he even smoked a cigarette.

"Rather wonderful, Barbara," he said. "The crowd, I mean. I've never seen anything like it in front of Mabers – never! I thought of going to America to pick up a few business hints. Marcus is rather keen on it. But I think I'll stay. I saw a novelty line in chemisettes over in Paris that ought to knock 'em dead." He beamed at her.

"You're not going to sell the business?"

"Sell nothing," said Mr Maber, whose association with Marcus Elbury had left its effects. "Besides, it's not mine to sell – not all of it."

He thought a second, debated the term in his mind, and then: "Kid," he added.

Barbara knew that the regeneration of Mr William Ebenezer Maber was nearly complete. There was youth in his eye, buoyancy in the set of his shoulders. Two days of prison had broken the ground; two days in Paris had produced a fertile crop of that quality which is described in one comprehensive word of American origin – a word that has not been used in this narrative. Mr Maber was alive, young, good-looking. Woe to the susceptible hearts of the golden-headed goddesses in the silks department!

EDGAR WALLACE

BIG FOOT

Footprints and a dead woman bring together Superintendent Minton and the amateur sleuth Mr Cardew. Who is the man in the shrubbery? Who is the singer of the haunting Moorish tune? Why is Hannah Shaw so determined to go to Pawsy, 'a dog lonely place' she had previously detested? Death lurks in the dark and someone must solve the mystery before BIG FOOT strikes again, in a yet more fiendish manner.

BONES IN LONDON

The new Managing Director of Schemes Ltd has an elegant London office and a theatrically dressed assistant – however Bones, as he is better known, is bored. Luckily there is a slump in the shipping market and it is not long before Joe and Fred Pole pay Bones a visit. They are totally unprepared for Bones' unnerving style of doing business, unprepared for his unique style of innocent and endearing mischief.

Edgar Wallace

Bones of the River

'Taking the little paper from the pigeon's leg, Hamilton saw it was from Sanders and marked URGENT. *Send Bones instantly to Lujamalababa… Arrest and bring to head-quarters the witch doctor.*'

It is a time when the world's most powerful nations are vying for colonial honour, a time of trading steamers and tribal chiefs. In the mysterious African territories administered by Commissioner Sanders, Bones persistently manages to create his own unique style of innocent and endearing mischief.

The Daffodil Mystery

When Mr Thomas Lyne, poet, poseur and owner of Lyne's Emporium insults a cashier, Odette Rider, she resigns. Having summoned detective Jack Tarling to investigate another employee, Mr Milburgh, Lyne now changes his plans. Tarling and his Chinese companion refuse to become involved. They pay a visit to Odette's flat. In the hall Tarling meets Sam, convicted felon and protégé of Lyne. Next morning Tarling discovers a body. The hands are crossed on the breast, adorned with a handful of daffodils.

EDGAR WALLACE

THE JOKER

While the millionaire Stratford Harlow is in Princetown, not only does he meet with his lawyer Mr Ellenbury but he gets his first glimpse of the beautiful Aileen Rivers, niece of the actor and convicted felon Arthur Ingle. When Aileen is involved in a car accident on the Thames Embankment, the driver is James Carlton of Scotland Yard. Later that evening Carlton gets a call. It is Aileen. She needs help.

THE SQUARE EMERALD
(USA: THE GIRL FROM SCOTLAND YARD)

'Suicide on the left,' says Chief Inspector Coldwell pleasantly, as he and Leslie Maughan stride along the Thames Embankment during a brutally cold night. A gaunt figure is sprawled across the parapet. But Coldwell soon discovers that Peter Dawlish, fresh out of prison for forgery, is not considering suicide but murder. Coldwell suspects Druze as the intended victim. Maughan disagrees. If Druze dies, she says, 'It will be because he does not love children!'

OTHER TITLES BY EDGAR WALLACE AVAILABLE DIRECT
FROM HOUSE OF STRATUS

Quantity	£	$(US)	$(CAN)	€
THE ADMIRABLE CARFEW	6.99	12.95	19.95	13.50
THE ANGEL OF TERROR	6.99	12.95	19.95	13.50
THE AVENGER				
(USA: THE HAIRY ARM)	6.99	12.95	19.95	13.50
BIG FOOT	6.99	12.95	19.95	13.50
THE BLACK ABBOT	6.99	12.95	19.95	13.50
BONES	6.99	12.95	19.95	13.50
BONES IN LONDON	6.99	12.95	19.95	13.50
BONES OF THE RIVER	6.99	12.95	19.95	13.50
THE CLUE OF THE NEW PIN	6.99	12.95	19.95	13.50
THE CLUE OF THE SILVER KEY	6.99	12.95	19.95	13.50
THE CLUE OF THE TWISTED CANDLE	6.99	12.95	19.95	13.50
THE COAT OF ARMS				
(USA: THE ARRANWAYS MYSTERY)	6.99	12.95	19.95	13.50
THE COUNCIL OF JUSTICE	6.99	12.95	19.95	13.50
THE CRIMSON CIRCLE	6.99	12.95	19.95	13.50
THE DAFFODIL MYSTERY	6.99	12.95	19.95	13.50
THE DARK EYES OF LONDON				
(USA: THE CROAKERS)	6.99	12.95	19.95	13.50
THE DAUGHTERS OF THE NIGHT	6.99	12.95	19.95	13.50
A DEBT DISCHARGED	6.99	12.95	19.95	13.50
THE DEVIL MAN	6.99	12.95	19.95	13.50
THE DOOR WITH SEVEN LOCKS	6.99	12.95	19.95	13.50
THE DUKE IN THE SUBURBS	6.99	12.95	19.95	13.50
THE FACE IN THE NIGHT	6.99	12.95	19.95	13.50
THE FEATHERED SERPENT	6.99	12.95	19.95	13.50
THE FLYING SQUAD	6.99	12.95	19.95	13.50
THE FORGER				
(USA: THE CLEVER ONE)	6.99	12.95	19.95	13.50
THE FOUR JUST MEN	6.99	12.95	19.95	13.50
FOUR SQUARE JANE	6.99	12.95	19.95	13.50
THE FOURTH PLAGUE	6.99	12.95	19.95	13.50

ALL HOUSE OF STRATUS BOOKS ARE AVAILABLE FROM GOOD BOOKSHOPS
OR DIRECT FROM THE PUBLISHER:

Internet: **www.houseofstratus.com** including author interviews, reviews, features.

Email: **sales@houseofstratus.com** please quote author, title and credit card details.

OTHER TITLES BY EDGAR WALLACE AVAILABLE DIRECT
FROM HOUSE OF STRATUS

Quantity	£	$(US)	$(CAN)	€
THE FRIGHTENED LADY	6.99	12.95	19.95	13.50
GOOD EVANS	6.99	12.95	19.95	13.50
THE HAND OF POWER	6.99	12.95	19.95	13.50
THE IRON GRIP	6.99	12.95	19.95	13.50
THE JOKER				
(USA: THE COLOSSUS)	6.99	12.95	19.95	13.50
THE JUST MEN OF CORDOVA	6.99	12.95	19.95	13.50
THE KEEPERS OF THE KING'S PEACE	6.99	12.95	19.95	13.50
THE LAW OF THE FOUR JUST MEN	6.99	12.95	19.95	13.50
THE LONE HOUSE MYSTERY	6.99	12.95	19.95	13.50
THE MAN WHO BOUGHT LONDON	6.99	12.95	19.95	13.50
THE MAN WHO KNEW	6.99	12.95	19.95	13.50
THE MAN WHO WAS NOBODY	6.99	12.95	19.95	13.50
THE MIND OF MR J G REEDER (USA:				
THE MURDER BOOK OF J G REEDER)	6.99	12.95	19.95	13.50
MORE EDUCATED EVANS	6.99	12.95	19.95	13.50
MR J G REEDER RETURNS				
(USA: MR REEDER RETURNS)	6.99	12.95	19.95	13.50
MR JUSTICE MAXELL	6.99	12.95	19.95	13.50
RED ACES	6.99	12.95	19.95	13.50
ROOM 13	6.99	12.95	19.95	13.50
SANDERS	6.99	12.95	19.95	13.50
SANDERS OF THE RIVER	6.99	12.95	19.95	13.50
THE SINISTER MAN	6.99	12.95	19.95	13.50
THE SQUARE EMERALD (USA: THE				
GIRL FROM SCOTLAND YARD)	6.99	12.95	19.95	13.50
THE THREE JUST MEN	6.99	12.95	19.95	13.50
THE THREE OAK MYSTERY	6.99	12.95	19.95	13.50
THE TRAITOR'S GATE	6.99	12.95	19.95	13.50
WHEN THE GANGS CAME TO LONDON	6.99	12.95	19.95	13.50

Order Line: UK: 0800 169 1780,
              USA: 1 800 509 9942
              INTERNATIONAL: +44 (0) 20 7494 6400 (UK)
                       or +01 212 218 7649
              (please quote author, title, and credit card details.)

Send to: House of Stratus Sales Department   House of Stratus Inc.
              24c Old Burlington Street   Suite 210
              London   1270 Avenue of the Americas
              W1X 1RL   New York • NY 10020
              UK   USA

PAYMENT

Please tick currency you wish to use:

☐ £ (Sterling)   ☐ $ (US)   ☐ $ (CAN)   ☐ € (Euros)

Allow for shipping costs charged per order plus an amount per book as set out in the tables below:

CURRENCY/DESTINATION

	£(Sterling)	$(US)	$(CAN)	€(Euros)
Cost per order				
UK	1.50	2.25	3.50	2.50
Europe	3.00	4.50	6.75	5.00
North America	3.00	3.50	5.25	5.00
Rest of World	3.00	4.50	6.75	5.00
Additional cost per book				
UK	0.50	0.75	1.15	0.85
Europe	1.00	1.50	2.25	1.70
North America	1.00	1.00	1.50	1.70
Rest of World	1.50	2.25	3.50	3.00

PLEASE SEND CHEQUE OR INTERNATIONAL MONEY ORDER.
payable to: STRATUS HOLDINGS plc or HOUSE OF STRATUS INC. or card payment as indicated

STERLING EXAMPLE

Cost of book(s):..................... Example: 3 x books at £6.99 each: £20.97
Cost of order: .... Example: £1.50 (Delivery to UK address)
Additional cost per book:.............. Example: 3 x £0.50: £1.50
Order total including shipping:.......... Example: £23.97

VISA, MASTERCARD, SWITCH, AMEX:

☐ ☐ ☐ ☐ ☐ ☐ ☐ ☐ ☐ ☐ ☐ ☐ ☐ ☐ ☐ ☐ ☐ ☐ ☐ ☐

Issue number (Switch only):

☐☐☐

Start Date: **Expiry Date:**

☐☐/☐☐   ☐☐/☐☐

Signature: _____

NAME: _____

ADDRESS: _____

COUNTRY: _____

ZIP/POSTCODE: _____

Please allow 28 days for delivery. Despatch normally within 48 hours.

Prices subject to change without notice.
Please tick box if you do not wish to receive any additional information. ☐

House of Stratus publishes many other titles in this genre; please check our website (**www.houseofstratus.com**) for more details.